CHRISTINA STEAD, a third-generation Australian, was born in Sydney and later lived in London and Paris. She worked for a bank in Paris in the late twenties. From that experience she drew much of the information she used so skillfully in her celebrated novel HOUSE OF ALL NATIONS. During the thirties and early forties, she lived in the United States, the setting of her novel THE MAN WHO LOVED CHILDREN. For a period she wrote for movies in Hollywood. Her other novels include DARK PLACES OF THE HEART, THE PUZZLE-HEADED GIRL, and FOR LOVE ALONE. She now lives near Sydney, Australia.

THE LITTLE HOTEL

CHRISTINA STEAD

 A BARD BOOK/PUBLISHED BY AVON BOOKS

AVON BOOKS
A division of
The Hearst Corporation
959 Eighth Avenue
New York, New York 10019

Copyright © 1973 by Christina Stead
Published by arrangement with Holt, Rinehart & Winston
Library of Congress Catalog Card Number: 74-6943
ISBN: 0-380-48389-0

First Bard Printing, February, 1980

BARD IS A TRADEMARK OF THE HEARST CORPORATION
AND IS REGISTERED IN MANY COUNTRIES AROUND THE
WORLD, MARCA REGISTRADA, HECHO EN U.S.A.

Printed in the U.S.A.

For Gunnvor and Oliver Stallybrass

If you knew what happens in the hotel every day! Not a day passes but something happens. Yesterday afternoon a woman rang me up from Geneva and told me her daughter-in-law died. The woman stayed here twice. We became very friendly, though I always felt there was something she was keeping to herself. I never knew whether she was divorced, widowed or separated. The first time, she talked about her son Gerard. Later, Gerard married. There was something; for she used to telephone from Geneva, crying and saying she had to talk to a friend. I was looking for a friend too. I am always looking for one; for I never had one since I lost my girlhood friend Edith, who married a German exile and after the peace went to live in East Berlin with him. But I can't say I felt really friendly with this woman in Geneva; I didn't know enough about her. My girl friend Edith and I never had any secrets from each other. We lived in neighboring streets. We would telephone each other as soon as we got up in the morning. On Saturdays we rushed through our household jobs to see each other; we rang up all day long and wrote letters to each other when we were separated by the holidays. Oh, I was so happy in those days. When you grow up and marry, there is a shadow over everything; you can never really be happy again, it seems to me. Besides, with the servants to manage, the menus to type out, the marketing to do, the guests to control and keep in good humor, the accounts, I haven't the time to spend half an hour on the telephone, as I used to. I used to dread this telephone call from Geneva. Still, if a person needs me I must talk to her, mustn't I? You never know. People live year after year in a hotel like this. We have their police papers, we know their sicknesses and family troubles; people come to confide in you. They tell you things they would not tell their own parents and friends, not even their lawyers and doctors.

This woman used to telephone me every day, while her son was engaged and making his wedding arrangements and when he left her house with his bride. I knew everything that was going on.

Then for a few months I almost forgot about them. One day she telephoned and said that her son and daughter-in-law, Nicole, had moved in with her. She was laughing and crying; nothing so tragic and yet so beautiful had ever happened to her, she said; and then again, she began to telephone me nearly every day about the young couple. I don't know what went on. It was never clear, except that she talked so much about happiness and unhappiness, love and misunderstanding, that I began to dread hearing the phone ring. I had not the time; you know I have headaches, I am worried about my husband Roger; and also I felt that there was something weighing on her which she could not tell me.

Yesterday afternoon, when I heard her voice, my heart nearly stopped. She was actually crying and said something terrible had just happened. She was sobbing into the phone and said she had to tell me before she called the police. She cried and exclaimed and said, "It had to come." I think she said Nicole was dead and Gerard her son had gone away and left her; but it may have been that her son was dead, too. Or that Gerard was dead because her daughter-in-law had hung herself. And at one moment I thought she said that Gerard had killed Nicole. But would she tell me a thing of that sort? You see, she speaks French very fast to me and as I am from German Switzerland originally, my French is bad. I have not had time to look in the paper this morning. Besides, I always fancied that I did not know her full name. Of course, she filled in her police papers; but though I keep in with the police, who are good friends of ours, I, on principle, do not inquire too far. The police are there for that; and then when, in the business, you are obliged to know so much about so many people, it is as well not to know too much.

The police are our friends, we need each other. My husband

Roger sometimes meets them in cellarings in the evenings; and we can always manage when any irregularities occur. Irregularities are a nuisance with the staff; but they matter hardly at all with the guests, who are here merely to amuse themselves and spend money.

Just when this telephone call came from Geneva, I was having trouble with a man who came here last week and asked to look at rooms. I quoted him the usual price, which is put up outside the gate, four-fifty a day for the room; and he said that was all right. He had breakfast in his room, ate two full meals in the dining room and for a whole week amused himself by walking around the town, and taking a bottle of beer to bed with him late at night. Yesterday, that made a week you see, he came down forty minutes before his train time and refused to pay his bill because he said I had given him an all-in rate of four-fifty a day. He had calculated to the last franc and had just the money for his train fare. I said: "I don't care about that. You must pay for your meals and wine and beer, not to mention service. Besides, I know you have more money than you say."

You may have noticed him in the dining room; a dark thickset man with a well-fed look, a businessman, probably—he said he came from Berne. No doubt he did. I don't like Berne people. They can never forget that once they were our overlords. He was coarse and stiff-necked in manner. He called me a thief and said he would send for the police. However, Clara the housekeeper had already gone for the police and they appeared much sooner than he wished to see them. They said, "Let's have no more trouble with you; or we'll put it into the record." They made him empty his wallet and there was not only enough to pay but nearly two hundred francs over. He paid all in the end and the police saw him to the station.

But in other instances the police leave the guests alone. There was the Mayor of B. Oh, what fun he was! He came about two months ago when Roger was away doing his yearly military service. He is a reservist. A limousine with a Belgian number and a liveried chauffeur let a man down at our gate, with a few pieces of baggage, and drove straight off. The man brought his own bags into the hotel and in a very pleasant way asked for the best room. He said he had stopped at our gates, because of our name, Hotel Swiss-Touring; he was in Switzerland and on a tour and he laughed. I gave him the only large room vacant. He filled in his police papers and it was then that he told me that he was the

Mayor of B., the Belgian city, and had come here for treatment. He had had a nervous breakdown because of drinking and eating too much; and too many beautiful girls, he said, and too many Germans. He not only filled in the police papers but made several notes on them.

At first the Mayor of B. took his meals in the dining room and before the meal went from table to table shaking hands, talking about the weather and other things. On the second day he began to complain about Germans in the dining room, though there was no one there resembling a German but Clara the housekeeper who was doing dining room service that day. One evening soon after, he started his meal, but after the soup came to me with his napkin in his hand, saying he must eat upstairs; he would not sit down with Germans.

I said Clara the housekeeper came from near Zurich and was a Swiss; and Madame Blaise, who I admit had been making a great scene over dinner, was no more German than he was. She was from Basel and the Basel people had resisted the Germans always. As for the other two guests,—a mother and daughter, Dutch from Leyden. The little girl had eaten cooked roots and gone without milk during the German occupation and was on her way to Villars, a health resort not far from us which is chiefly for the tubercular, though we do not use that word.

The Mayor of B. was very pleasant, but said he would not risk the germ contact with Germans; and he was ever after served in his room. He twitted me, harped on Germans. He several times came upon me speaking German to Clara the house-keeper; he asked me, Who is this German woman? I said, She is not German but Swiss and she is my housekeeper. She won't like you calling her German. There are no Germans here. During the war we had Germans but now there are none.

"Ha-ha," he said, "but every day I see cars outside with German numbers. I see them from my balcony." Those are Americans, I said: there are no Germans here. Then he began doing such funny things. We all had a good laugh. Luisa the chambermaid brought me down a hand-towel marked with the hotel name. He had written in ink round the border—I can show you. I was so amused, I kept it; one should always keep certain things. He wrote:

If this is a sample of the towel you give guests in the Hotel Swiss-Touring (and his writing was arranged to

*take in the woven name, you see) it is no wonder that
guests who are short of writing paper use it; for there is
no writing paper supplied in the Hotel Swiss-Touring;
so that if guests want to write letters or complain about
the GERMANS in the place, they will be sure to look
for materials and to write on towels and tablecloths, so
take notice. Signed, the Mayor of B.*

And he sent this towel down to the office and marked it
Document 116; he had marked his police paper *Document 101.*
The other documents in between had been some messages on old
envelopes and a bundle of view-cards provided in the
writing-room, which he had sent out to be posted. We had
posted them, including the price of the cards and postage on his
bill. He always paid his bills without question and promptly. As
far as that went, he was a pleasure to know, openhanded and
honest. He even sent one of the cards to me with the following
words:

*Document 112: To Madame Bonnard at the Hotel
Swiss-Touring. Certificate from the Mayor of B.
Madame Bonnard, bonart, bonnarr, (that means good
fool), Anyone who wants to visit your hotel can apply
to me, Hotel Swiss-Touring. I am the Mayor of B. and
I am well satisfied with this hotel. I like all the Germans
it contains, down with Germans, why do you have
Germans in your nothell? Down with Germans, down
with hotelism, Madam Bonnarr is a very good
German, a b c d e f, ach-german, boo-german,
cousin-german, down-with-german, eat-with-german,
fooey-german, germ-german. Heil, Madame Bonnar!
Get out the Germans and I will come and drink
champagne with you. Signed, the Mayor of B.
Document 112.*

Then the maids began to bring me towels and pieces of paper he
had written upon. He himself brought me a bundle of papers to
put in the office safe. "Top secret," he said, "top secret." He
winked and held up his finger. "I have brought all the
incriminating papers away. I have come here to get cured and
those left behind will have a headache!"

Every day there was something new with the Mayor. It kept

the guests amused. They did not complain so much. Every day he went out and bought four bottles of champagne. After a few days he bought a season ticket to Zurich which is our largest business city. They say it has the same amount of traffic as New York; and what a lot of big cars! There he had important business. He is a trustee, he says, and is buying large properties there; he's putting Belgian money into them. But he went to Zurich only a few times and then he started to take the boat to Evian, in France. At first I thought he went for the casino; but he only went there to get champagne which is cheaper in France than here. Every day he brought back a dozen of champagne.

He invited all the hotel servants to drink with him and everyone had his health drunk; but he never invited the guests. He gave me four bottles for ourselves. Roger and I accepted one bottle in the beginning and drank it with him. He gave the toast of Down with all Germans and Swiss-Germans, which was difficult for me since I am German-Swiss as he knows; but he made us laugh so much that I did not really mind. Then the next day he said: "I have a whole crate of champagne for you. I must go upstairs and bring it down. Send up two of your servants to help me." It turned out that it was a miniature crate of liqueur chocolates shaped like champagne bottles. But up in the room, meanwhile, he drank the healths of the two servants, Clara the housekeeper and Arnold the porter's boy.

Most days he also went up the hill to the clinic. There he received his injections and shock treatments. When he came back, he always came first into my office and said: "Too much of a good thing! Any more of it and I'd fall down dead at his feet, on the floor of the clinic." But he said he was feeling better.

He had arrived dressed in a style some people think right for Switzerland, tartan shirt, open neck, soiled pair of trousers, of good make, leather jacket, muffler, cap and beach shoes.

He paid his bill regularly and without any objections; but he always wrote underneath something like this: *Bill paid to the Germans, seen and approved, the Mayor of B. Document 127* or whatever it was.

I was uneasy about him, especially as the weather was still wintry, sharp, and he kept crossing the lake to Evian without an overcoat. After I mentioned it to him, he wore his wool muffler; he even wore it to the W.C. And then he began going to the W.C. without a dressing gown or slippers, but in his pajamas, hat and muffler. He told me not to worry: the mountain wind was good

12

for his headache. "I have a headache every night all night; it comes from the fever."

The Mayor became a nuisance, ringing the bells all day for the staff, insisting upon attendance. He would have two or three of them at a time in his room, haranguing them about business, explaining how they must wait upon him; and next, amusing them, doing balancing tricks and forcing them to drink champagne. He would close the door and I would hear shouting and shrieks of laughter. I had to forbid them to stay in the room when the door was closed; and said there was to be no more than one of them in the room at any time. For the next thing might be that he would get angry with them, very high-and-mighty, he would chase them out saying that he must have better service or he would leave. Then he would storm down to me, only half dressed, asking for clean linen or pen and ink, or saying the food tasted bad.

To begin with we had very little linen and we were just starting to build up our supply; and then our laundress was good but slow. She has a little laundry business of her own which she runs with her son. But she is very nervous and does not sleep at night because she is afraid the Russians will come in with their troops and take her business. One day she was so sick in the stomach that she could not bring the linen but sent her son, who is even slower than she is. Another day, there was a strike; yet another time the weather was very wet; and so on. I sent the Italian sisters, Luisa and Lina, to help her with the laundry; but they are not experienced, though great workers. So quite often the housekeeper would be short of clean linen. The Mayor would come out into the corridor, cajole her, try to take clean linen out of the cupboard when she had it open. Lina was often sitting in the little sewing room behind the office; but you could hear the sewing machine going and in he would go, whenever I was out of the office, joking, commanding and trying to take the clean linen she was mending on the machine. Then he would examine the sheets to see if they were mended; and say, "I cannot sleep in mended sheets." Anything, you see, to cause excitement. Yet he was an amusing interesting clever man. I liked him even though he kept on calling me German. Roger, of course, saw him with different eyes. In the end he telephoned the Town Hall of B. He could not tell whom he spoke to, but he was told that our Mayor, though not the Mayor, was a very high official; and Roger got the impression in a few minutes' conversation that it was better not to inquire too much; better to leave things as they were. Roger, though inquisitive and suspicious, is prudent; and so we did leave it at that.

Such scenes would take place in the morning, say. Then the Mayor would go off somewhere to Zurich or Evian-les-Bains or to his doctor. He never went to Geneva which is the nearest of all, because, he said, you met too many international types there, spies, globetrotters, who might recognize him; and he was here incognito. If in the hotel, he would dodge in and out of his room and the office talking to me or playing with my little boy, Olivier. The Mayor told me it wouldn't be safe for him to hold too much property in his own name and he had so much now that he had to give some of it away. For one thing he would have to pay too many taxes; and then if the Russians came in he would be considered a bourgeois and stood up against a wall and shot. At this he would laugh loudly. Or, the Russians might just allot him one room in the back of the hotel, and where would be his advantage? He was always calculating how long it would take the Russians to occupy Belgium—seventeen hours at the most. He laughed a lot and did not seem to care; and he used to comfort us and laugh at the other guests who thought the Russians might drop in any day. Roger did not like this. He likes to take things seriously.

People would gather round when the Mayor started to talk about the Swiss mountains, the foreign gold hidden there and what the Russians would do with it. All the guests became excited and Madame Blaise, who is from Basel, a rich town in a flat watery country, would say the Russians particularly wanted the flat country, the Rhine valley and the waterway to the sea; while Mrs. Powell, the old American woman, would raise the dust about "the Swiss trading with the enemy"; and Madame Blaise would say roughly: "Why don't the Americans use the atom bomb on the Russians now? A surprise attack. What are they playing games for? Mrs. Trollope, an English lady who had spent all her life in the East, would say quite unexpected things, such as:

"I don't see why the Russians wouldn't win. We are always shouting all our secrets from the housetops. They only have to wait."

Mrs. Powell, who was partly deaf, would say to me, in her loud rough way: "There are communists even in this country, in

14

Switzerland. Why don't you get busy and stand them all up against a wall?"

To this everyone would agree, except the Mayor, who had been in a position of authority; and who would laugh at everyone, though why I never was sure. Naturally, he hated the Russians, but he would listen to each one with a quizzing smile; suddenly you would see a profound smile crease his face; and he would begin to laugh aloud. For example, on one occasion, Madame Blaise said she had it all planned. Her son was in New York, she herself had a lot of property in New York; she liked America and she was going to hire a plane and fly off. She said: "In any case, I have to go. I have millions lying there in different banks and I must make them give it back. That is why my son is there, waiting for me." At this moment the Mayor smiled profoundly, as if he had discovered a case of champagne; he burst out laughing. Madame Blaise seemed a large fat goose; don't misunderstand me, I think she was a very cunning, very clever and very rich woman, but being a heavy rude selfish woman she was not quick to take a hint; so she simply went on saying:

"The Americans are not such fine people; don't think they care for us and our problems. For them it's Number One; let them get their paws on our money and they stick to it. I have been fighting for years to get my money back and it is still sequestered. You see, it was war conditions; it could not be put in people's own names; they had to trust Swiss people; and some of us did not know, so we put it into the U.S.A. Supposing Switzerland were invaded; why would they want our mountains? For the money! We are the richest country on earth. Why should we have all this worry? We must protect ourselves. So you see," (she said to Mrs. Powell) "You should not think only of self, but you should see the Russians destroyed, because it is to your interest too. If we go down where will you be? All Europe is your buffer state."

"Not the English: you have a socialist government; you are collaborators with the Russians," said Mrs. Powell turning accusingly to Mrs. Trollope.

Roger and I used to get them to disband as soon as we could; they all agree in hating the Russians but they began to dispute, each blaming the other for their present worries. I had time to think that if Madame Blaise had property sequestered in

15

America, since she is not an enemy alien, but a Swiss, then that property must have been enemy alien property entrusted to her, which she was now claiming. She would not be the first one. During the war many Swiss took charge of German property to prevent its being confiscated; some did it for kindness, others made a profit.

One evening the Mayor said he would draw up a document giving his property in Zurich to my five-year-old son Olivier. It was only a temporary document, not witnessed or properly drawn, but he labelled it *Document 157.* He said we must call it between ourselves Document 157; never mention it to Roger and never refer to it when with others; and he told me to put it away in the safe. My safe was getting full.

Apart from the Mayor's papers, I had a parcel of jewels belonging to Madame Blaise and a packet containing thousands of Swiss francs and American dollars belonging to Mrs. Trollope and her cousin Mr. Wilkins. Madame Blaise would examine her jewels from time to time, for, she said, with Italians about, there was no security; then she would do it up again ready to fly with her to America.

Mrs. Trollope's parcel was a source of worry too. It was labelled *Property of Robert A. Wilkins,* which was the name of Mrs. Trollope's cousin, but the money it contained belonged to Mrs. Trollope. I never knew why it was there; for they had bank accounts in the local banks. But Mrs. Trollope would come to me almost every day talking about it, crying about how short of money she was. Supposing something happened to Mr. Wilkins, "which God forbid"? The odd thing about this was that Mrs. Trollope was an heiress, richer than her cousin. That was a mixed-up story. Mrs. Trollope told me everything and I soon understood; yet you are always astonished at how people can muddle their lives.

Most of our guests are in bed by eleven, a middle-aged set. But we have a year-long contract with the local nightclub, the Toucan, to lodge their touring artists and we put up the road companies who play the Casino. The artists for the Zig-Zag Club are a poorer crowd and put up in working-class pensions. We like the Toucan people. They are well-behaved and some of them come back each season. They get up at five or six in the evening, have coffee and rolls, lunch at the nightclub and eat a snack in their rooms before going to bed. About this time there came back to us Lola-la-Môme, who does apache and South

American and other dances. She is forty-two, short, strong and plump with thick black hair which she dresses like a savage; and she is still healthy and sexy enough to get applause doing bellydances and acrobatics with her partner. Her manager is her husband, who is a few years younger; and her partner is her lover and about twenty-five. The three of them go about together and are quite famous. They quarrel and fight in public, but never here. The husband doesn't like his position but can't afford to lose Lola-la-Môme and her partner. But Lola insists upon picking up rich tourists in the nightclub. It is dull enough here, let us admit it, at night; and all the places but nightclubs close at midnight. We're a Calvinist country, very gaitered and neckbanded, parsonical. So after twelve the rich tourists resident in neighboring towns have only the Toucan and the Zig-Zag and sometimes the Casino to go to. When Lola suggests bringing the men home, the men are eager, you can't blame them. When her partner or her husband object, she says she will leave the act; and she has left them once or twice.

She explained to me that I had no idea how dull it was living with two men who are always putting up with each other, and holding on to her; and I could understand. I told her she ought to live with just one man like I do; it is more difficult and you are never sure you can hold him. Lola thinks she can get a rich lover any time she wants to; that is an illusion, I suppose.

Lola is a vulgar woman who wants to get money out of these rich tourists. I forbade them to dance in the house; they just talk, drink and make love. It is all upstairs out of sight on the top floor. The artists get reduced rates, so they live in the smallest rooms and you can imagine that in so small a space it gets stuffy; the people often quarrel. The night porter has to watch them and go up and knock on the door. Then Lola-la-Môme comes out and says she is just having a party. We can hardly prevent stage people from staying up at night after their work; and after one warning Lola usually cools down for the rest of the season. She does not want to go and live and eat in the working-class pensions where people go to sleep early and nothing of that sort would be permitted. Most of our guests know nothing whatever about Lola unless they go to the nightclub.

But how could you prevent the Mayor from knowing? He went to the Toucan many evenings. He bought drinks for Lola and her family and came home with them. They started to sit up all night and since the Mayor does not concede that they have to

17

work, but pretends they are out for a good time, we had him running up and down the stairs and wildly about all night, singing and executing funny little acts on the carpet-runner on the landing. Some of our guests slept through it all; others became curious. Not to explain further, the Mayor began to do a striptease in order to dance an apache dance with Lola, although Lola told him over and over, and I believe this, that the male apache does not have to be naked to dance. She does a striptease at the club and ends her dance in nothing but a few beads, as my father used to say.

Mrs. Trollope said: "I have never seen anything quite like Lola's act; it's unnecessary to go so far, though it is a nightclub. And Mr. Wilkins and I are broadminded; we have seen a good deal."

I began to wish the Mayor would move to another hotel. We have had troublesome guests before and the servants can always get rid of them without anything having to be said by me. For instance, we had the Admiral here. She was an old Englishwoman who must have been a society beauty. Her fine white hair was always done as if a maid had done it and in it she wore at dinner a pale blue velvet crescent set with pearls. She had magnificent blue eyes, her skin was soft and her flesh so firm that everyone thought her about sixty-five. She was really eighty-two. Her voice had broken, she was deaf and had aristocratic manners, abrupt, overbearing or suddenly sweet and conciliating.

We had a new electric lift which had just been installed and was always being adjusted. The engineer had to come several times from Zurich.

She walked with a stick and would call out from the landing in her clear correct English French: "I am old, I must have the lift. Make the engineer operate it for me."

When no one came she would bellow: "Eh, the man up there, eh, the housekeeper! Where are the domestics?"

It is true that this was at mealtimes; but it was also intentional that no one came near her till she had been shouting there for ten minutes or so. I used to stand at the bottom of the lift shaft listening, until people began to come out of the dining room to laugh or sympathize. Then I would send Clara up to her. This woman was not worse than others; but the staff did not like her. They would not serve her, so all I could do was to help them to get rid of her. She sat at the little table that all the old women like; the chair-back is against the radiator. Usually there was no menu on her table. She would not wear glasses and so she could not read the menu that was always on the gate and in the lift. The waitresses knew this. They would hold the menu up to her and then whisk it away.

"Give it to me, give it to me," she would call. The waitress would come again, and put it down on the tablecloth in front of her; and as she bent slowly over the waitress would pick it up and hand it to someone else at another table saying, "Yes, certainly, Madame, here is the menu."

Now "the Admiral" would study the menu card in the lift, but the new lift went so fast that she had no time; and whoever was in the lift would disturb her to prevent her reading, saying, "Have you room enough, Madame? Is Madame well today? Here we are, Madame," and so on, so that she never could study it. Everyone of us laughed at these little tricks; but it was not healthy laughter as with the Mayor, the kind that keeps the servants cheerful. As a result of their petty venom, they became disturbed, they hated her the more.

They would leave her sitting there, beautiful for her age, grand and noble, flushing like a peach with humiliation. When she had ordered her food, they would bring it up cold and she would eat it cold to avoid another scene. Most of the people, Swiss and others, laughed at her: she just fitted in with their old-fashioned ideas of the out-of-date English milords.

She was poor, yet she complained. She did not like it that the same woman who cleaned her room put her soup in front of her.

"A chambermaid does not serve food." She did nothing unreasonable but she did not consider the low rates she was paying. "Pity them, the English are so poor now, the most unfortunate people on earth," my Papa says, "and yet they cannot lose their pride, their tradition, their history." I told Papa that nothing can be done when servants have made up their minds to get rid of someone. You see, she gave no tips: she paid her ten percent service, but nothing extra. The servants are very poor and need the little extra. As it is, on their days out, you will find them sitting each by himself eating a roll perhaps, on the seats along the promenade getting a little fresh air and waiting to go home to sleep. We do not feed them on their days out. Very often too they spend the day in bed, eating a little bread or fruit. You see most of them send money home to their families, and their families think of them as the rich ones. Well, it is not the business of the guests to worry about that and not mine either; we must all live and eat, and out of the same pot. The way they see it is, there are people living in comfort, doing nothing and eating all day, who deny them a few extra pence. Yet I have seen them very kind to certain guests who do not pay extra; it is a question of luck and personality.

This Englishwoman was unlucky. She was obliged to leave and went to a place along the esplanade just up the hill, much less convenient for her, since she had a stiff climb from the lake-front; and there I know she is just as badly treated, for after a while all their servants learned the joke from our servants.

Good. You see the servants found the Mayor amusing and he was good to them. They began to get tired of him, though, when he woke them up at night. I forbade them to attend to him. Just the same he found out their doors and knocked on them, both at night and during the afternoon rest hour. I told him not to.

One day soon after this he asked for Document 157 back and his other documents too. He said they were false, fraudulent, poisoned documents and would do him and me a lot of harm: they were illegal and must be drawn up afresh; and in place of these he gave me a signed receipt, Document 158. He never lost count and his documents seemed quite legal to us. Roger was worried, but he had no excuse to go in and look through his luggage. This is absolutely forbidden to hotel keepers in Switzerland; and though we do it when we are desperate and afraid of being cheated, we do not like to. Roger, also, wears rubber soles and controls the guests by listening on the stairs, on the landings or in an empty room where he pretends to be shifting furniture, examining the radiator or feeling the floorboards for rot. The water and heat pipes act as a telephone and the air is so still and the guests usually so quiet that there is little we miss, especially in the off seasons. Roger would have made a good secret-service man. He was born in French Switzerland but in an upland valley close to the German side. He was miserably poor, very ambitious and went first to Zurich to a German hotel, since when he has always believed in the Germans as a serious, highly educated, orderly people. It was there that he learned the value of being documented about everyone. "You never know," he says. Yet it is for himself: there is a strong nugget of obstinacy and independence in him which prevents him from talebearing to our police. "They're paid for it; let them get it for themselves," he says. I am very thankful for this: to tell the truth the other is very like spying. Some of the guests come upon Roger when he is spying; that is the way I put it, to annoy him.

One day Mrs. Trollope came down to see me, and after beating about the bush she asked if Roger was ill: he seemed strange. They had noticed him walking around muttering in the dark places of the landing; he stood for a long time on the stairs near their doors, making believe to polish the railings with his bare hand. She said to me nervously: "This morning he was standing in the dark outside our doors, and when I came out unexpectedly he went silently as a ghost down the side corridor and opened the door of one of the empty rooms; and he spoke into the room. He said, "Is everything all right, Madame?" But I knew there was no one there, for I had just been looking for Clara to give her a skirt. I went back into our rooms and told Mr. Wilkins to look out of his door. He looked and saw Mr. Bonnard pulling the lever on the radiator outside our room back and forth. When he saw Mr. Wilkins, he cleared his throat and said, "I believe we shall have to take the heating off and fix the boilers." Mr. Wilkins came in and I went out a few minutes later to the bathroom; and there was your husband on the floor near my door, tapping with his finger at a floorboard. This is very upsetting, Madame, to Mr. Wilkins and me."

In excuse, I told her about the Mayor who was quite a poser for Roger. The Mayor said to us this morning: "If any Belgians come here you will let me know, won't you? I don't want to see them. I am here incognito and I don't want people to think I am ill. I am a very well-known man." He followed this with the usual document which he this time called: *Memorandum to Madame German Bonnard*.

Mrs. Trollope said with much interest, "You don't suppose that he has something to hide?"

I said we were watching the papers to see if any scandal was blowing up. They were still shooting collaborators in Belgium. It was very strange the amount of money he had; he washed his hands in it, threw it out of the windows. Yet he received letters from firms and lawyers in Zurich addressed to the name he had given, and underneath always, "Mayor of A."

I teased him: "Why do they call you the Mayor of A. when you are the Mayor of B.?"

"It is because I am here incognito," he explained.

If the letter was not addressed to the Mayor of A. he sent it back.

One of Roger's nervous fits was coming on. He chain-smokes

and spies more when he is going to have a fit of the blues. As for me I was glad to have the Mayor, who now occupied two adjoining rooms. He said he must have a bedroom and a study.

The morning this arrangement was made, he rang all the bells, assembled the whole staff and showed a pair of shoes, one shoe outside each door.

"Those shoes are not to be touched; I have staked my claim."

We sent up the bill; he paid it at once. He insisted however upon keeping the pair of shoes in their position outside the doors. He said, "In case you are tempted to give the rooms to another German family."

"That was a Greek family."

So far, all was easy. We had at that moment only five permanent guests in the hotel. There was Mrs. Trollope and her cousin Mr. Wilkins, English people from the East, who had been with us for over a year and who occupied two adjoining rooms. On the same floor, next to Mrs. Trollope was Madame Blaise, who had been with us the whole winter. Next to her was the large corner room, a double bedroom with a fine view, which Dr. Blaise occupied every second weekend when he came over from Basel.

On the other side of Mr. Wilkins at this moment was Miss Abbey-Chillard, an Englishwoman who was a great worry to us. A custom began during and after the war of allowing some English people to stay on at the hotels with only promises to pay, for it was felt that ordinary exchanges would soon be re-established and the English visitors would be allowed to pay their bills in Switzerland. Switzerland received many English visitors in the old days. The English like to come away and stay in a place for a long time. For example there was a couple, a Major and his wife, seen every day along the esplanade, who had been on this part of the lake shore for over forty-five years. They were beginning to worry about dying among foreigners; but they were afraid to go home for they believed the Labor Government would enroll them at the labor exchanges and send the man out to work on the roads, since he had no occupation. These were fancies they had among themselves.

Thus Miss Abbey-Chillard was troublesome; but one never knows; a hotel keeper cannot be too cynical or harsh. People who do nothing for a number of years are naturally eccentric. Miss Abbey-Chillard wanted invalid dishes and wished to pay less for them because they contained no meat. At first she ate in the dining room and then in her room, and we had too few servants for that. Her meals often enough were brought back untouched; and then she did not want to pay anything for "this beastly swill."

Francis the French cook would howl when he heard what she wanted for lunch; and I or one of the girls would prepare the soup or milk dish on a small burner. Hence, it was not always very good.

Then Madame Blaise, who had poor mountain girls to work for her in Basel, expected abject servility. She always quarreled with Rosa, a maid we then had from Lucerne who was a schoolteacher's daughter and had come to learn French. Educated servants are always more difficult than the others. Madame Blaise and Rosa quarreled in public. Rosa tramped and swirled round the dining room, pleasant to some, rude to others. Madame Blaise, sitting at the table, as always, in her jacket and dress and even in fur coat, with her big hat and bags and shawls hung round the chairs, made service difficult. Rosa took advantage: she shoved Madame Blaise and spilled the dishes on her shawls. Madame Blaise took advantage: she sent back the dishes three or four times. While all this was going on in the dining room, Francis the chef, a very nervous and proud man, would be creating scenes with the Italians and Germans. One day Gennaro, who had been scrubbing the floors, had to peel the vegetables. He took hot water in a basin in the kitchen and washed his arms up to the elbows in it. Francis was just coming in to prepare lunch. He instantly flew into a temper saying he would not tolerate dirty—I leave you to imagine—Italians washing off their dirt in his kitchen. Gennaro trembled: "There is no hot water in my room." I came in and the Italian girls came in to support Gennaro: there was a noise and I threatened to send for the police and send Gennaro to the frontier. Francis said, as usual, that he wold cook no lunch. He agreed to do it at length only if the dirty Italians worked elsewhere. I had to get Clara to help with the vegetables. All the Italians were mad with rage; the atmosphere was frightful; a silent uproar was going on all round me. In the meantime I had to make sure lunch was ready at the usual time for the guests who were as usual spending the morning walking up and down waiting for their food. At this very moment I found the old porter Charlie staggering upstairs to the attic with a bed. "What are you doing, Charlie?"

"The Mayor wants one room for his study and says I must take this bed to the attic."

"Take it back this instant. Mr. Bonnard and I alone have the right to have the furniture moved. The idea of guests moving furniture! Take it right back."

He grinned grimaces, said: "What can I do with a circus number like that? What a card! You could run a whole circus with just one number like that!"

He turned slowly round, shouldering the bed, and crept downstairs. Charlie is sixty-five, a real Frenchman, who has sailed all around the world. He is getting too old for his work, but he's been a very strong man and he's reliable and has sense. He has a very bad police record and is always going up there to answer some charge or other—the fact is, it's a quiet sort of joke we have; even Mrs. Trollope and Madame Blaise found out about it. They are close friends and spend many days together. They were walking along on a shopping tour in Lausanne, one afternoon, when they saw Charlie going into a shabby little hotel with a schoolgirl. We could not help giggling together when they came back and told me. One of these days he will go too far. The very next week, the father of a twelve-year-old girl came rushing down here with a stick; and Charlie has already spent three months in jail, for a thing like that. But he's a decent man, knows everything about hotel life, he's well broken in, a clever old Frenchman, who no doubt is not very anxious to return to France. He understands all the guests and they rely on him. There is something very soothing about the intelligence of a broken good-natured old scamp: and then he's a poor old man. What has he to look forward to? He'll end up on the roads; and be picked up and go to jail again.

He and Clara and Luisa the Italian girl with her sister Lina, who's tubercular, though I never say so to guests, form an old guard upon whom I can always rely. The only surprise I got that afternoon was when Lina, a good Catholic girl, and a married woman, led a little spearhead of Italian servants into my office and said, The Italians must not be treated like dogs: I must make Francis behave or get rid of him.

And at the very moment I was scolding Charlie for moving the bed, Mrs. Trollope came up from lunch and said:

"Oh, Madame, I see you have been thinking about my sciatica: for I see that this bed does not sag in the middle."

24

I had quite a scene with her while everything was explained, and I had to get very cross with her too. And what happens at this very moment? Naturally, the telephone rings in the office and the woman from Geneva speaks to me and tells me she expects every moment to be arrested.

When Mrs. Trollope found that the bed was not for her, she went crying to her friend Madame Blaise. They were on good terms at that moment; and the next thing I knew was that Madame Blaise had moved her chaise lounge into Mrs. Trollope's room. I flew into a temper at that, and scolded them both. I was really furious. It's simple. To keep order in a hotel, everything must stay in the same place; and then there's the logic of equality. If one guest has new linen curtains, the other must have the best of the older curtains; if one guest has a new plush armchair, the other must have a cane lounge; if one has an extra table to write on, the other must have a footstool. I sometimes let Charlie fetch things from the attic or even from my own room to be sure of this equality; but I cannot allow others to make changes; I have a plan of it all in my mind. Take the cane lounge in Mrs. Trollope's room. The next time the two women quarreled, Madame Blaise would come down to me and shout that I groveled to the English and trampled on the Germans (she being like myself, Swiss-German), because I allowed Mrs. Trollope to have a plush armchair and a cane lounge; and that this was because the Germans lost the war owing to the intervention of the Jews, and that Mrs. Trollope was most likely a Jew. I am very firm. It is the only way to manage these disorderly people. They are just like spoiled children. It's funny, isn't it? Here I am, only twenty-six, and I am running men and women of forty, fifty, sixty and seventy, like schoolchildren. The secret is simple. You must have your own rules. We have another simple secret. Our hotel, the Swiss-Touring, which is near the station and near the esplanade, is the cheapest hotel in town for visitors. Cheaper than us are only the workmen's pensions and students' lodging houses. No one ever mentions this fact, among our guests; but it is this thing that keeps them from boiling over.

They are counting their pennies. They have some money, some are rich, all are getting on and getting anxious about their years; and besides them there are a few poor travelers, people without a home who go from one cheap place to another, all over Europe; there are some refugees now settled with us; some collaborators who escaped in time after the war; then the nightclub people and, in winter, the people going up to the snowfields.

Mrs. Powell was there for the first time then. She had taken a house in another canton, in Thun, and then gave it up when she found out she had to pay heavy residence taxes. Mrs. Powell had the little table near the radiator. This table was next to the corner table occupied by Mrs. Trollope and Mr. Wilkins. Mr. Wilkins sat with his back to the wall and under a large mirror. They both could look out upon Acacia Passage and the gardens of the next villa. We kept the side-shutters closed in really cold weather, with long curtains; in those early days we had old curtains which had come to us with the hotel. Mrs. Trollope sat facing Mr. Wilkins and the mirror in which she saw reflected all the guests in the dining room, and the kitchen when the service door or the trapdoor opened. She spent a good deal of the mealtime looking into it. She slept badly on account of her sciatica and had stomach pains due to her nervousness. She ate very lightly and very often would not finish her soup or her salad. Mr. Wilkins spent most of his mealtimes reading the *Financial Times,* the *Spectator* or some popular book on science or politics. Mrs. Trollope felt humiliated and complained; but he did just as he pleased and answered either with a derisive smile or a remark such as, "I assure you no one notices it, Lilia, but yourself."

If he was not reading, Mrs. Trollope would talk about her diet or the new car Mr. Wilkins wanted her to buy. She did not want to buy it. She was tired of traveling and she was afraid of motoring in such mountainous country. Mr. Wilkins said, "Very well, we shall strap a coffin to the roof."

Sometimes, when he opened his book, she would go up to her room at once, saying that she had a headache or that her back was aching. Mr. Wilkins would rise politely as she left the table and would tranquilly go back to his reading. On these occasions he would stay at the table and read till they were clearing the tables. Mrs. Trollope was very sensitive to appearances. If she came down first, she would go and sit at the neighboring round table, occupied by Madame Blaise. If she saw that Mr. Wilkins had already come down and was reading, she would go to their table, say a few polite words to him and go and sit with Madame

Blaise, dawdle there till half the meal had passed. We never served a guest at another guest's table. When Mrs. Trollope's soup came to her table Mr. Wilkins would call, after a moment:

"Lilia, do come and get your soup; it will be quite cold."

Usually she would go to him, sometimes not. He would go back to his reading. She would play with her soup and, when the meat came, say:

"Robert, please pay some attention to me. Madame Blaise says I should drink herb tea; what do you think?"

"Madame Blaise is not a doctor. I don't know how you have become such a faddist, Lilia."

And that afternoon she would have herb tea at four o'clock with Madame Blaise; though at seven she and Mr. Wilkins had their usual whisky and soda. Another time she ate meat dishes for a whole week because Robert suggested that it was hunger that was keeping her awake. Again she said to Robert:

"Mrs. Powell said perhaps I need some mental activity; but I told her I always finished the crossword puzzle before I went to bed; and that the solutions kept me awake in the night."

Sometimes he would not answer at all, but with a superior air go on reading; or would remark with his cool and charming laugh, something like:

"There was only one copy of the *Financial Times* at the stand and the Major and I reached for it at the same time. We both laughed and I said, 'Please take it, Major!' But he said, 'Not at all! Let me glance over it, if you will be so kind, and then I shall be satisfied.'" And he laughed. The Major was this resident who dressed in plusfours and lined gaiters. He belonged to the old community of English in town which never acknowledged English visitors. Mr. Wilkins was of a small middle-class family in Yorkshire and was snubbed and ignored by the resident English, even those drunk or in debt. If, however, Mr. Wilkins talked about what was in the *Financial Times,* Mrs. Trollope was interested and gave him advice. She was a lightning calculator and had great business sense; yet she did not want to do anything with it.

Mr. Wilkins got up early in the morning, about seven, got out his sheets and prepared his daily chart, for analysis of the currency fluctuations and stock market quotations. He would say with a smile:

"You see, I can tell you the quotations anywhere in the world at a glance now."

27

When he had to go to the bank to change a check, he went armed with these figures; but he pretended (if they did not know him) to be an ignorant British tourist, to see if the exchange man would give him a tourist rate. Then he would tell acquaintances about it and become indignant: he might threaten to change his bank; then he would lay his plans for another exchange operation. If nothing occurred, and with his *Financial Times* in the pocket of his well-worn overcoat, he would dawdle along the esplanade, watch the workmen, study the timetable to Evian, read an old geography he borrowed from our library. The gardeners would be rooting up, setting, netting against the birds, the fishermen would be painting and mending boats, lake scows would be discharging pebbles and boulders, laborers tipping stones along the lake-front to protect the lake wall. In spring come squalls and floods; there are washaways. At this time, too, they were repairing the road down beyond the tin factory; they had pneumatic drills, steamrollers, barrels of tar along the wharves and boat-sheds. Mr. Wilkins would come back smiling to lunch:

"I get real amusement out of watching the men at work."

Then he would be pleasant to his wife and talk to her. By his wife I mean Mrs. Trollope. I am sure they were not cousins; and we all thought of them as husband and wife; but for reasons of his own Mr. Wilkins kept up the transparent comedy.

Half an hour after lunch, he would go to sleep, and sleep till the sun descending shone into his room from across the lake. Then he would get up, take a walk and put out the things for their whisky and soda.

Mrs. Trollope did not sleep. She went to the Catholic church, and went shopping and to tea with Madame Blaise; and when she came home she was consoled.

"The real reason I can't sleep, Robert, is that I have nothing to do."

"Why do you want to do anything, Lilia? We are retired," said Mr. Wilkins.

"I am going to ask them at the church if there isn't something I can do."

"I hope you are not going to make us ridiculous, Lilia. Please remember the absurd Nice affair."

Mrs. Trollope grew desperate and told me everything. When they had been staying in Nice two years before, she had absented herself every afternoon while Robert slept; until Robert, who

28

had got up early from his nap, saw her wheeling an old woman in an invalid chair, into a pharmacy. Mr. Wilkins prudently pretended not to see her; but that night he found out that she had answered an advertisement and become companion for a wealthy invalid.

"Does she pay you?"

"I use the money for myself. You are always asking me what I want it for."

"You are disgracing us.".

"What harm did I do, Robert?"

"Surely you can see how very absurd you make me look! You will give this up at once, Lilia. Remember, we are retired, now."

"I shall die of boredom! Supposing we live to be eighty? I am sick with boredom."

One day I found her in the dining room helping Clara polish the tables. I made her some tea myself and sent one of the maids into the sitting room with it; and then I told her it was bad for discipline.

It's easy to see why she made so much of even a horrible person like Madame Blaise; though I suppose I should not speak that way of the unfortunate woman. When Dr. Blaise came on his weekends, Mrs. Trollope was always at their table and so eager for fun that she did not notice Dr. Blaise's impatient smiles, glances, shrugs. These fits of intimacy, especially at the weekends, were always followed by tiffs between the two women; and all these events were so routine that no one noticed them. It was necessary for Dr. Blaise to come every two weeks, for he brought his wife the supply of drugs she needed; if he did not come, she was wretched. The Blaises had much to keep them together, a daughter, a son, Madame Blaise's fortune, a beautiful old house in Basel. And notwithstanding all that went on, Mr. Wilkins and Mrs. Trollope were devoted and could not live without each other.

But I want to finish about the Mayor of B. I mentioned that Number 29 at that time was Mrs. Powell, the old American woman. She married a Washington official at the age of nineteen; she was now seventy-eight and her husband had died thirty-nine years before. She inherited from him a small fortune and at once began to travel. She had scarcely seen the United States since. She lived in hotels, sometimes took a villa, moved from place to place, always avoiding the income tax. She looked many years younger than seventy-eight; she was round-cheeked.

blue-eyed, with a delicate skin. She was able to dress in powder blue, pale rose, cream, and looked pretty with flowers in her hat or on her shoulder. She walked smartly. Seen from the hotel, as she tripped along the promenade, she might have been in her thirties. She was a little deaf but not so deaf as she said. She showed her age only by a heavy snoring which could be heard all over that part of the house, and in our bedroom through the hot water pipes: and perhaps by her dabbling in mischief. At first she was agreeable and interesting.

She and the Dutch ladies frequently talked about backward peoples. One of the Dutch ladies said:

"Naturally, backward peoples need administrators; the clash between their old tradition and our modern one is too great; the one crumbles and the other is a hardship. They need us to find the way out for them."

Mrs. Powell was very much concerned about race itself. She was from the South, she told the Dutch ladies. She was modern, she did not believe in what she called southern talk; but she had very strong ideas about races.

"You see, I understand them. It isn't right to mix the races. You see a lot of them married to other races here in Europe. I've seen it everywhere. People here say it makes no difference, but I feel something when I see it. Now if there was nothing, if it did not shock, I wouldn't notice, would I? But everyone feels a sort of shock. Don't you feel a shock?"

"Well, one thinks about it."

"Now that is not natural. You see there hasn't been enough time. Now that is one argument I had with Mr. Roosevelt, but he was such an egotist, so much wanted his own way that he wanted to realize everything in his own lifetime. That's unreasonable and egotistic: it takes generations. Were the Roosevelts made in a day? I asked him. And the same thing is true of others, of Jews. A lot of them are very pleasant at first; they have fine manners, you like them and they seem very bright; but it soon breaks down and they have ways you feel are different."

"But the Jews are older than we are," said the younger Dutch lady.

Mrs. Powell paid no attention.

"It's, as I see it, a question of generations. Now James Truslow Adams, you may have heard of him, says something like this, that one of the disasters of the war between the States was that all that fine flower was destroyed and that is one of the reasons for the troubles and confusions we see today. And Darwin showed that God has arranged it so that blood will tell. I have seen a good deal over here, I have seen some who have got through, and what is the result? You see it all about you, this disorder, this ruin of the fine old culture. Not only they but other races have got through; and how can we go back to the time before, when that has happened? No one would approve of Hitler, but he understood the danger. He pointed it out; but very few people took any notice. It's unworkable, he said; it simply doesn't work. Now I cannot approve of the extermination of peoples and yet you might say he was like a surgeon cutting out the disease. Yes, people have seen it, Darwin saw it, he was of a fine old family; but we of the good families are too few. Everywhere you turn, in every street, almost in every hotel, in this hotel, you will find some of them. But it's unworkable. It will break down. Our culture will break down and the Russians come in. Unless what few of the old cultured people are left will get together and bring order into this confusion, however hard it may be and go against our feelings. We must make a stand and do something whenever and wherever we see it."

I did not know at that time that Mrs. Powell had a purpose; and Roger was very much impressed by this. He had no education, a poor farmer's boy from a stone farm—that is, a farm covered with stones. He thinks the Germans are very clever: they gave him his first chance. "You were very clever, not the Germans," I say; "you are a funny kind of French boy." He gets very morose and angry at this. As for me, I laughed to myself about all that the old fools were saying. Chemistry and physics do not seep in through generations but are learned in school in four or five years. Americans come from a new country though: their views are strange and original. Ideas are not very important to them; it is their own aim that counts. I learned this from Mrs. Powell. I did not know her nature then. She had been away from her country for nearly forty years and yet she was the most exaggerated American I ever knew. How could I guess that Mrs. Powell was beginning a campaign to get rid of Mrs. Trollope, and that she thought about it at night and carried out her plans in the daytime?

On the third floor the rooms were rather small. Number 31 is the corner room kept for Dr. Blaise on alternate weekends. Number 30 is the one Madame Blaise has all the year round. The one opposite, Number 32, was occupied by Mrs. Powell, who thus lived opposite all four. These rooms, all but Number 32, face the lake and they are connected by a whole series of communicating doors so that if necessary a whole family could take a suite; we had a Greek family which did so.

At night Mrs. Powell's snoring had an intermittent roar; it was like a seaside geyser; you could hear the sucking and the gurgle. Madame Blaise came to me and wanted Mrs. Powell moved. Mrs. Powell did not want to pay more; and did not want to go up to the fourth floor where the rooms are for artists and skiers. Madame Blaise was rude to Mrs. Powell. Mrs. Powell at once approached Mrs. Trollope:

"I am afraid I bother you with my snoring."

Mrs. Trollope said, "Oh, no, not at all; I assure you not at all."

Mrs. Powell soon began giving out cuttings from newspapers and magazines about the Russians and American policy. It's better not to read the books and papers guests give you; besides, I had no time and my English is not very good. I gave them back with that excuse. One was a magazine with a gaudy picture of Karl Marx on the cover and a description of his ideas inside; and of his insides too. I think it said that he was a revolutionary because of his liver trouble. This magazine appeared an hour later in Mrs. Trollope's letterbox. Mrs. Trollope took it upstairs and before dinnertime it was returned to Mrs. Powell's letterbox with a note pinned to it. They met outside the dining room door as they waited for the bell.

"What did you think of the article?" said Mrs. Powell, who spoke loudly in her deafness.

"I don't understand politics," said Mrs. Trollope.

"What did you say?"

"I don't understand politics," shouted Mrs. Trollope.

"You don't want to talk in public?" inquired Mrs. Powell.

Mrs. Trollope was the same height as Mrs. Powell; both were very small women. She bent towards the old lady and said sharply and slowly:

"Don't like politics."

The old woman looked her straight in the eye and said:

"Last night you said you approved of the British Labor Government!"

Mrs. Trollope stared at her and then turned to me. I stepped forward and asked the ladies about their health. Mrs. Powell answered that her health was always very good and she went. Mrs. Trollope said:

"Well, I think her hearing must be good, too. What I said last night to my cousin was that the Labor Government was doing its duty in trying to save the pound."

Mrs. Trollope went into the dining room and sat in her place with her back to the room. It was a rainy day, the shutters on the ragged damp gardens were shut and the lights were on. I had my work to do and went round to the service kitchen. Clara was waiting on table that day. She is a lively woman and likes fun. Mrs. Powell with a grimace, part wink and part smile, placed her magazine at the little round table at the other side of the room where the Dutch lady sat waiting for her daughter. She walked trimly across the room, nodded to the girl at the table beside her, and herself sat down with her back to the radiator. She had begun her soup and was lifting a spoonful to her mouth when she froze as it were, shivered all over. Her eyes opened, her jaws shut fast, she put down the spoon and seemed about to rise. Instead, she watched with a singular intentness a young Negro dancer, ready to go out to work, who had come in and who went to her seat at the back of the dining room. At the back we kept little tables where the artists from the Toucan could sit among themselves unobtrusively. They always behaved very quietly. There were two more Negroes, one man and one woman in the act with her: they were from the French colonies. Mrs. Powell sat quite still and staring and only after a long pause put the soup again to her mouth. When the younger Dutch lady came in, Mrs. Powell tried to attract her notice, but the older lady having said something to the younger, they took care not to catch her eye; and they seemed to have some slight joke between them. Madame Blaise had come in. Mrs. Trollope, who had seen everything in the mirror, got up excitedly and went over to her friend's table. Mrs. Powell's gaze, still incredulous, moved from the dark-skinned artists to the others in the room and she even looked for sympathy to Mrs. Trollope; but Mrs. Trollope was too busy with her friend.

Mrs. Trollope and Mr. Wilkins slept a good deal in the daytime and so they often went to the Toucan or the Casino to drink and dance after dinner. You don't have to dress to go to the Toucan or the Casino, just simple afternoon frocks or suits. They hobnobbed with all the artists and would often drink with them. It was rather expensive, said Mrs. Trollope, but then she and her cousin liked a good time. Mrs. Trollope was always quite eager to talk to the artists and would smile and "bow" as she said, that is incline her head, when they came in; and she did this now. Mrs. Powell fixed her outraged glance on Mrs. Trollope's face. When dinner was finished Mrs. Powell came to me in the office and said:

"You said when you're busy in summer you turn that little writing room into a dining room for the extra table?"

"Yes."

"I think the dancers at the cabaret would be happier if they had a place to themselves. They don't eat at the same time, they eat differently, and they must feel out of place with us."

"They are quite happy, Mrs. Powell. With our system of separate tables, which is so different from so many hotel-pensions, everyone keeps to himself. Mr. Bonnard and I are very proud of having separate tables instead of long tables which you will find in other hotels at our rates."

Mrs. Powell went upstairs, put on her hat and went out for a brief walk. From then on she made a detour when she entered the dining room, to say hello to the Dutch ladies and straight from there to her own table. Thus she avoided Madame Blaise who had complained about her snores, and Mrs. Trollope whom she now called nothing else but "that Asiatic."

I laughed the first time. "She is not an Asiatic."

The old woman insisted: "She is not one of us: you don't feel she's like you and me."

"She was very beautiful as a girl, I've seen a photograph."

"They often have a showy prettiness when they're young; that's one of the signs."

"But she's as white as you or me," I said; though I knew and everyone knew that Mrs. Trollope had something strange, foreign, which I thought very interesting in her pale-skinned face.

"White! With those eyes," said Mrs. Powell.

Mrs. Trollope had beautiful long dark eyelashes and not a gray hair. She dressed this fine black hair in a crown or aureole. She had thickened and coarsened, but her wrists and hands, her ankles and feet remained delicate; and she was always shopping for shoes small enough to fit her. On the nails of her small pale oval hands she wore pale pink enamel, and they made me think often of a bush we have along the esplanade, the flowering judas. In early spring when the first green buds appear on other trees, this bush puts out pale rose sessile buds, the size of rice. She and Madame Blaise would sit together on the esplanade and when I passed sometimes out walking with Olivier I would see them, holding each other's hands. Madame Blaise's were heavy, knotty and thick with rings: Mrs. Trollope's were veined but reminded me of these bushes. She also wore many rings, thin rings of different colors and a good many bracelets going up her arm. The two were fond of jewelry. They would often go shopping for jewelry, visit all the expensive jewelers in Lausanne and Montreux, get a powder-case, a lighter, get a ring mended, substitute a more expensive movement in a wristwatch for the old one, have their initials put on things, buy a handbag. Then they would spend days saying they didn't care for the things and in the end change one or several for others still more expensive.

So they would sit talking in low voices, explaining about their rings and their children. It was a touching sight, their aged hands on their laps. I would think of them living in a foreign town, unhappy with their men, away from their children. They were mothers and both were very rich. What had they but a tiny room in a fourth-class hotel? That's how we're classified.

How Mrs. Trollope came to be there, I'll explain later on. Madame Blaise blew in one morning in a fuss and said she would never set foot in her house in Basel again if she lived to be a hundred. She was staying here and the Doctor could come and plead, she was staying here forever.

"Who knows what a doctor can do to you? A doctor can do anything, even in your sleep," she said, and she was speaking of her husband Dr. Blaise, a very well-known practitioner.

About this time there were several cases of stealing in the hotel. Mrs. Trollope and Mr. Wilkins never locked their doors. Mrs. Trollope explained, "We trust the servants; never have we locked our doors." But most of the others locked their doors. Madame Blaise had a door into Mrs. Trollope's room which was never locked, and the door between the rooms of the "cousins," as we called them, was always open. One day Mrs. Trollope came down to lunch early, leaving her door ajar and her big crocodile handbag on the plush armchair, facing the door. Mr. Wilkins came to the table immediately afterwards, and a few minutes later Madame Blaise came down. She was as usual dressed in hat, jacket, coat, scarf and with her handbag, which she never let out of her sight.

Mr. Wilkins was reading a book about nuclear fission. He kept showing bits to Mrs. Trollope. She turned her face away and said:

"Robert, I should have a better appetite if you paid attention to me at meals. We are not made to eat like pigs from a trough."

He said in his starched way, laying down his book:

"I cannot very well eat your food for you, can I, Lilia?"

I was at the serving hatch. I should have laughed if Roger had said that to me, but Mrs. Trollope burst into tears and went upstairs, though for once Madame Blaise stirred herself and called,

"Liliali, Liliali, come and sit with me."

"Oh, I can't, Gliesli, I am too unhappy; I must bear my sorrows alone." Out she trotted weeping and said to me:

"Oh, Ma-dame, if you only knew, but may you never know! You have your good husband and your little one with you!"

Mr. Wilkins read, and Madame Blaise ate more deliberately than ever. In the afternoon, instead of the usual quiet, which I take advantage of to do my accounts, there was some running about and discussion. I looked through the brass lift-cage upwards and saw Mrs. Powell standing in the corridor, while Madame Blaise was in Mrs. Trollope's room turning things upside down and Mr. Wilkins was standing in his own doorway, saying crossly:

"You're so careless with money, Lilia! You'll probably find it in one of your pockets."

I went up and Mrs. Trollope ran out to me.

"Oh, Ma-dame, I have lost a hundred-franc note. You know I always keep one in my purse."

She then described how she had left things, the door ajar, almost wide open, and she said:

"There's a strange-looking man I don't like at all who is always creeping up and downstairs with a briefcase, an underhand kind of man who tries to avoid notice and looks as if he would be glad of money."

Madame Blaise said: "It is that dark man who flirts with Clara."

But the man in question was the accountant who was in to look over my accounts.

"And there is another man, who keeps to his room, he shuts himself up and does not eat with us. He lurks about the stairs."

I said: "That is Herr Altstadt. He is most respectable."

Mrs. Powell said that the Belgian Mayor had locked himself in the bathroom since before lunch. She had knocked at the door, but it had remained obstinately shut.

I called Charlie, the old porter. He came laughing.

"Yes, what a card he is! He's been sitting in the bathroom crying for three hours. I spoke to him through the door. He won't say anything but this, 'How miserable I am, what a rascal I am, I owe my misfortunes to myself.' "

I told Charlie to get him out at once. The Mayor had just paid his bill, but perhaps he was cleaned out and could not go out for his champagne.

Charlie and I called out in turn, "Mr. Mayor, come out, we're all friends here, come out. What is the matter?"

But he wasn't crying then, he was laughing and I thought he might have taken the money. He might have wanted to play a trick on them. At that moment Luisa the chambermaid came upstairs and said:

"Poor man, oh, poor man. I am sure he is in trouble. He was crying all the morning. I knocked at the door and said, 'What is the matter, Mr. Mayor? I will help you.' But he went on weeping."

We all three knocked, but now he sat there laughing to himself and humming a song. I felt sorry. My heart was touched. I said:

"Come out, Mr. Mayor. There is someone here wants to see you."

I thought he might be drunk. At these words he was quiet. Then he said in a strange tone:

"Who are they?"

We were all silent, reflecting. Then Luisa said:

"Mr. Mayor, it is only the employees of the hotel who wish to thank you for your goodness to them. You know me, Luisa!"

She whispered to Clara, "Go on, go quickly! Get some flowers out of the dining room."

But they were only dried up everlastings which had been there the whole winter.

Mrs. Trollope quickly unpinned her violets and gave them to Luisa.

Suddenly the Mayor called: "Charlie! Very well, Charlie, go and get me some clothes. I have nothing on. I can't receive people like this."

Charlie winked. "How the devil did he get there?"

Charlie got a dressing gown, hat, muffler and shoes. The door was unlocked, Charlie handed in the clothes and the Mayor came out dressed in hat, muffler, sunglasses, dressing gown but with his shoes in his hand.

Said Charlie: "You see, he wore his sunglasses at any rate."

"These shoes must stand in front of the doors of my suite," said the Mayor severely and replaced them.

His feet were well shaped, pale, clean. He was, in fact, a good-looking man in all ways.

Luisa gave him the violets, making a speech to him in Italian. He smiled. At his door, the Mayor turned and cried:

"Champagne for all! Thank you, friends!" and then told Charlie to go for champagne. He comamnded:

"To the Hoirs! To the Hoirs! I like them. During the street fair they gave me twenty little bottles for nothing at all."

These twenty little sample bottles, wine and liqueurs, he had wrapped into a parcel, which he carried into the sewing room to give to Lina, "For the Italians, you understand."

It was as if a little bird had told him about the awful quarrel at that time between the Italians and the French cook. He was a very clever man, I know that.

The Hoirs he mentioned were just up the street. Charlie lost no time and came shuffling back with four bottles of champagne at eleven-fifty each. Well, to pay for it, the Mayor gave Charlie a hundred-franc note and there were some strange glances at that. But whose really was it?

Roger was now out frequently with friends in the town. When he returned this time, he got rid of the worry in his usual practical way; "The thief is either Mr. Wilkins or Madame Blaise, their doors are open into Mrs. Trollope's room. No servant would dare take so much. Mr. Wilkins would do it for discipline and Madame Blaise is a big spender. She despises Mrs. Trollope and everyone here. For that matter I myself despise rich people who live meanly in a fourth-class hotel."

"That doesn't mean you would steal from them."

"And she takes more drugs than the doctor brings her."

"How do you know that?"

He said no more.

A few days later, Luisa came to me about what we called the *forbici* affair. For days we heard about nothing but *i forbici*, which is Italian for scissors. For troubles of this sort we relied on Luisa's good sense. She was a thin brown-haired girl, and had come with Lina her sister who had had tuberculosis, was almost cured but wanted to work on the Lake of Geneva for her health. When I met the sisters, Lina was cured, and I took her in. We just had to conceal the state of her health from guests. There are a lot of walking cases and convalescents about; people must work and you have no trouble with them. They would not dare make trouble.

Lina works in the sewing room and never comes in contact with the guests. It is the younger one, Luisa whom I rely on. She sometimes makes friends of the guests, and she likes order kept among them. She scolds them, she smiles at them, she cries for their troubles if she likes them. If she takes an interest in a guest, not the same as liking but nearly, she tries to teach him Italian. "You must learn, come, listen, I'll teach you, it's easy. One word after another. Bu-on-gior-no! Buon-gior-no! Good-day! Buon giorno! Good morning! Say it, Madame, please."

The conversation you see was all in Italian except for the few English words she had learned herself. And all the time she talked she worked. In the morning she hurried to Mrs. Powell's little room and she could be heard saying:

"Aren't you going out, Madame, Ma-da-me? Sortir. Sortire." Sorr-tirr? Go-ah-oot? Sortire? It's lovely now. But, of course, Madame must learn Italian. I teach her. I-ta-li-a-no, Madame. Volete parlare italiano, Signora? Si?"

And she would apply herself, while she turned a mattress, shook out linen, dusted, to teaching one Italian word. Very early in the morning, about six, Roger and I studied English in the basement near the furnace while Gennaro or Charlie made up the furnace. Charlie knew English very well; Gennaro knew quite a bit too. There was a window on the narrow light-well and every word we said could be heard clear as birds at the top of the airshaft. Luisa leaned out of the window as she was dressing, catching the warm air and the English words.

Mrs. Powell was always losing things. Though she did not speak Italian and scarcely a word of French, she managed to let Luisa know about them. When Mrs. Powell went out for her walk Luisa would start moving furniture and looking for them. Mrs. Powell had mending bags, sachets, numerous paper parcels. She wrapped things up and tied them with ribbon or string and would have to unwrap them to see what was in them. Luisa begged her,

"Buy those plastic bags, Madame; you can see through them."

Luisa would see the little lady tripping in her pink and blue along the esplanade and would go through the room looking for what was lost. Afterwards Luisa would say in Italian:

"Supposing I packed for you a bit, Madame? Arranged things in drawers, eh? But of course you lose things like this. Perdere-è-facile. Lo-oose eezy! I arrange everything? She doesn't understand! Too bad."

Mrs. Powell cried out in her strong loud voice: "Luisa my stockings have been stolen! Vous compre-nay? Volay—volay, stolen."

"Si, si, Signora, leave it to me, ho capito," said Luisa very fast, but she would think it over before she really understood. To me she would say pettishly:

"Why can't she learn a few words?"

I explained to Luisa: "She says that she thinks it vulgar in Americans to go abroad and come back home and say words with a foreign accent."

Luisa cried, "Indeed, indeed! Then let me assure the lady that she is in no danger of being vulgar. Never. She is very elegant. The height of elegance."

And yet when Mrs. Powell at breakfast said, "One off, for my breakfast, one off with bacon, vous comprenay?" Luisa called "Oui, oui" with a smile and would say in the kitchen, "She is trying hard."

Luisa went on with her teaching efforts. "Sun, soleil, Madame, sole."

The deafish old woman cried, "Volay, volay, stolen; kelkun, someone, stole my scissors. The man. L'homme. Get l'homme. The new man on the stairs. The sulky one."

"De quoi? Che dice, Signora?"

"Volay, volay."

"Ho capito. Stockings, eh? Ha-ha. There they are!"

"No, no, scissors!"

"That's bad. I'll look. Behind the boxes. Feld down, eh?"

"No, no, pas tombay, volay, volay."

"No, no, pas volés, no stolen, feld down, Madame."

"My scissors! Volay. L'homme."

It took Luisa two days to find out what had been stolen this time. She came running up from the sewing room where it had come to her. She ran to Mrs. Powell.

"Signora! I understand! I forbici—click-click, like that, eh?"

"Yes, scissors."

"I forbici, allora, ah, i forbici."

For some reason Luisa became alarmed. She asked advice from Mrs. Trollope. Mrs. Trollope herself went down at ten-thirty at night to talk to Gennaro, who was on night duty. Gennaro was getting ready to lie down on the sofa. We were then trying out Herman, a new man from Lucerne. He was tall, dark, strong but sulky, lazy. He would look straight down into your eyes and wear a slight smile and then go away mumbling. Everyone but Clara disliked him. Luisa said to Mrs. Trollope, "I have an idea she is going to have our boxes searched, this Signora Powell."

Meanwhile, Clara was conspiring and flirting with the new man, Herman, on the quiet upper floors. Mrs. Powell had lost three pairs of nylon stockings, a silver-backed comb and the scissors. Herman, said he, stood up against the wall in the dark to watch her go to the toilet and rushed into her room when he heard the door close. Madame Blaise, too, said when she came from the W.C. she found Herman in the dark part of the hall, between the linen-cupboard and her room. Mrs. Trollope believed he looked through keyholes. She had been sitting in a certain place at a certain time, her clothes round her waist, when straight in front of her she had seen the strangest thing—a soft dark fringed living thing, a human eye in the keyhole. This Herman was an imp of disorder. I don't know that he did anything wrong, but he disturbed everyone. Herman's little room was on the top floor, between the lavatory and the bathroom. He was there when he should have been working, and in the legal rest-hour he was elsewhere. Mrs. Trollope said: "He is always skulking about. What can Clara find so interesting in him? Clara is such a refined woman. But then she is too good-hearted to be suspicious as we are."

I said: "Clara is not refined, Mrs. Trollope. This air she has is to fool you. She is a mischievous old maid and always hatching plots."

Well, Luisa found the stockings but not the scissors. Said Luisa:

"Something must be done. She is talking about the police. She's a regular bulldog: she'll never let go."

When I came upstairs there was Clara between two cupboards flashing her nails and taking something into Herman. She scurried away smiling and waving her hands to me. "Another German alliance," I thought to myself. Clara was a restless intriguer: she tried to get all the German-Swiss servants into her plots.

I called Herman down to the office and told him he must get on with the floors upstairs. Old dirt and wax made them dark. They had to be cleaned off with steel wool and rewaxed. Herman always got into a huff when told to work. He took his time about going upstairs and I heard no sound of scraping for half an hour, but I heard whispering. That was Clara again. They were both on the top floor near the servants' bedrooms. I went upstairs and met Clara coming down smirking. She had knitting needles in her hands which she was going to lend to Mrs. Trollope. At this moment I was short handed because Charlie had just taken to his bed with his floating kidney. The Italians were all muttering among themselves, saying *i forbici* and were slow at their work.

Later on that day, the scissors were found on Mrs. Powell's dressing table. Luisa said both to me and to Mrs. Powell: "I put them there; they were not lost."

More than that she would not say, not where, nor whether she had any suspicions, not even if Mrs. Powell herself had lost them. "Enough is enough."

After this, whenever Mrs. Powell lost anything, Luisa would say emphatically:

"Like the scissors, eh, Madame, like *i forbici?*"

I had a suspicion that Herman had taken them for some purpose; but I don't know.

That was the end of lost things with Mrs. Powell. She returned to her political work, which consisted in making cuttings about communism and putting them on the tables before meals, or in the letterboxes. She was the most patriotic American I ever met.

Mrs. Powell sat in the dining room and if Mr. Wilkins had not yet come down, but Mrs. Trollope was there, would make loud conversation about communists, to annoy Mrs. Trollope. She told a good many people that Mrs. Trollope was a communist. If she was, pigs have wings.

One night after such a scene, I invited Mrs. Trollope to the movies. The film was *Goodbye, Mr. Chips* and I was longing to see it. Mrs. Trollope wanted to see it again. She said:

"It gives you such a feeling of the dear old world still being with us in the new; though the young seem so old nowadays."

Just as Mrs. Trollope and I were talking about this in the office, Mrs. Powell went past with Clara. Luisa was putting my boy Olivier to bed and Clara was going to baby-sit and had her knitting under her arm.

Said Mrs. Powell to Clara:

"I never imagined there would be so many colored people and halfbreeds about in Switzerland. Communism attracts such unfortunates."

Clara was smirking and she winked at me.

Mrs. Powell continued: "I heard of one who was sent to a convent and married straight out of the convent young; that was before the color could show, of course. They very often have an exotic beauty when young, though they coarsen with age and you can see it then."

I closed the door and told Mrs. Trollope to come into the sewing room while I got ready. I had to lock up my desk. I would just say goodnight to Olivier and give Clara a stiff look to cool her down.

But Mrs. Trollope put her head on my shoulder:

"In the East, in Malaya, it never happened to me; they're much kinder in the East."

I stopped her by telling her about the new document the Mayor had given me. He was going to buy the Hotel Lake Leman, which is right on the lake and charges much higher prices. He was going to put the hotel in Olivier's name.

"I don't see why the Mayor should not want to make such a sweet little boy a gift to remember him by, especially if he is alone in the world," said Mrs. Trollope.

"As the Mayor is ill, he may suddenly have realized what it is to have no one to cry for you when you're gone. You come back and look at a tombstone and think, there is my dear father. Perhaps he might want Olivier to take his name as a second name. You ought to suggest that. After all, it is a really magnificent present."

I looked out. There was no one about but Clara, who was singing, croaking rather, a song to herself. Mrs. Trollope said, forgiving her:

"Clara is always so happy."

I got my hat on and when I went out Clara was sitting in her chair at the office door watching the stairs, the lift, knitting the same old sweater and chatting with Mrs. Trollope who was admiring her clumsy work.

"It is for my boyfriend," said Clara coyly.

I wondered in passing what she was so good natured about. Mrs. Trollope, like most people, was taken in by Clara's red and yellow cheerful face and the blonde mat like a wig piled on her head which, at fifty, had not a single gray hair in it. The sweater had been done for Christmas, but had such small armholes and neck that it was more fit for Olivier than for a man, and so it had to be undone. Clara, with nods, pokes, glances and stabs with her needle was indicating to Mrs. Trollope that she would be in charge of the house, while the proprietors were out enjoying themselves; that she was a motherly sort, who after working all day, found pleasure in staying at night to look after my child. I came and whisked Mrs. Trollope away. Robert Wilkins was downstairs talking with Charlie and drinking whisky with him; my husband had gone to another cellaring; this was becoming quite a habit of his. He pretended that it was good for business: in these cellarings he met all the influential men in town.

How good Clara was, said Mrs. Trollope, what a nice woman, one felt comfortable with her.

I said: "Clara is all right as long as she feels herself admired: she will play up to you. But she is treacherous, underhand, turbulent and a plotter."

"I thought she looked so happy and romantic knitting for her sweetheart and looking after your baby. I feel quite fond of her."

"You don't know her," I said, laughing gaily.

Now we were hurrying along the street in the damp mild air and I forgot all my troubles. "She's only happy when there's trouble and misery; and when there isn't she stirs people up until there is. She's full of smiles: something is cooking."

"But she has an honest straightforward jolly way and she's a hard worker."

"She thinks she's indispensable because she was here before us. On the other hand she conspires because she's afraid of her old age. You must beware of old servants, old horses and old dogs."

Mrs. Trollope sighed and said life was very cruel.

I was just telling Mrs. Trollope about the happy days when my girlfriend Edith and I went out every afternoon arm-in-arm, and how Roger and I had taken Edith in in her trouble at the sad time her parents put her into the street, when we passed the

Hotel Lake Leman. There were three men on the corner, one of them middle-sized, bareheaded and excited. It was the Mayor. He saw me and ran up saying: "It is done, it is done this very minute, Madame: the business is concluded."

He talked eagerly for a bit and we went on. I explained that he meant he had bought the Hotel Lake Leman. We gave it a quick glance as we hurried past, at the tiled entrance full of glass doors, palms and carpets. I had noticed that one of the two other men was the manager of the hotel. He did not acknowledge me. People were jealous of us when we first came here into the hotel business. They had driven others away.

Mrs. Trollope kept asking me about the Mayor and halfway through the film, when the break came, she made me quite a long speech in an undertone. She said, in the East, she and Mr. Wilkins had known someone rather like the Mayor. She said I must watch the servants and guests. He might wait for them in the dark and jump on them. I was surprised and interested. I had never seen a madman and I thought they made faces, howled and had fits. I could not help saying that only that morning the Mayor had had a long talk with me about Olivier and how we ought to train him if he was going to be an actor—for Olivier is always dressing up and loves to recite. The Mayor knew a lot. He had mixed in the very best society. He told things that made me laugh. A woman he had known in the very best society in Brussels had a lover who objected to her horsy teeth; so she had them all pulled out and her mouth remade. Just then her husband died and her lover married a high school girl. "I loved her for her wonderful teeth and she pulled them out," was his excuse. The Mayor said, "Belgian society is very amusing and very cruel; you would like it very much."

We liked the movie. Mrs. Trollope said she was glad to see a story of natural sweet little boys. After we had a quiet beer I told Mrs. Trollope about my troubles with Roger. There is a married woman after him, my best friend Julie, the one who keeps calling me German because I like beer. She makes him smoke and drink too much; and she leaves me alone with her husband while she goes off with Roger. She is French and she flatters Roger that he is truly French. Her husband, although he is Roger's best friend, tried to kiss me. Mrs. Trollope said to me, "This woman wants to make up a foursome." Until that evening I had never heard of such a thing. I said:

"But why does she insult me and Olivier so much? She said,

'Olivier used to be a beautiful child; now he is cross-eyed and fat and getting more like you every day.'"

Mrs. Trollope told me that the mother of a beautiful child must put up with a good deal of jealousy.

The next morning was Friday. There were only two or three people in the dining room for breakfast, people who had stayed overnight; and I let young Emma, Gennaro's wife, make the coffee. The cook Francis had left, I had a new cook coming; but in the interval I had the old German chef who had been here before, in Clara's young days in the hotel. He was an aged man, obliging, glad of the work. He got occasional work in the workmen's pensions and did odd jobs. His cooking was in the German country style, which our guests did not care for; but for a day or two it did no harm. He made good plain flour soups, boiled meat with potatoes and cabbage and desserts of flour and jam. And, unlike Francis, he got on with everyone.

Emma was an Italian mountain peasant, serious, goodlooking and very intelligent. I think she was the most intelligent of all our servants; and yet she knew nothing when she came to us. The Christmas before, I had allowed Gennaro to go to her home, to ask permission to marry her. He asked our advice several times: "Is it right? Am I fair to her? Is it the right thing to do? She is a young girl, only nineteen years old and I am compared with her an old man, thirty-four. Fifteen years is a great difference. I am not sure it is right."

But then he would add: "She is a very serious woman and I am serious. Her opinion is that it will work out. I asked my mother's advice and she thinks Emma is a good wife for me. My married brother and his wife, also, are in favor of it. They think I should marry and they overlook Emma's poverty. They say she herself is such a fine woman that they consider I am lucky."

At such moments he would change expression and say: "I'll tell you the truth: I think myself very lucky to have found such a fine woman. Her poverty is nothing to me."

Gennaro met his mother every morning when he was cleaning the lowest part of the building, which is almost on lake level. Since the hill is so steep, one side of the hotel is almost on lake level and the chief entrance is up the hill just below the station. The lower entrance is a wide calm place, very sunny in the mornings; Gennaro liked to work there and spend a few moments in the sun. His mother came past every morning on her

46

way to another little hotel where she worked as chambermaid; and there they would meet.

Emma was short and thickset but I could see her attractiveness. Roger came from the mountains himself and preferred town types. Gennaro, you see, was born on the lake shore here, at Nyon, and he had lived here all his life, except for the war and a few years as a child under Mussolini. His family came from the Borromean Islands. If you have ever seen them you know that those low-lying islands are heavenly. The grandfather's home was in these islands and Gennaro was saving money to buy it, so that his mother could go there in her old age. Therefore he thought a long time about marrying. What confused him more was that now his mother, a widow, wished to remarry. He was ashamed: "People will say I cannot provide for my mother."

Emma came to us with only a cotton dress. She had not even a shirt or drawers, nothing but her dress and a coat belonging to someone. Someone in the train had lent her a pair of bedroom slippers, high-sided plush shoes with a fur edging, to pass the frontier; and Gennaro found her barefooted at the station, when he went with his little handcart to pick up any tourists and to collect her luggage.

Gennaro left her in the waiting room at the station while he ran all the way downhill to the hotel, got his money, hurried back and bought her a pair of shoes in a shop up Great Oak Street; and so after several hours he brought her to us in a new pair of shoes; and I was very angry with Gennaro for dawdling. She had brought absolutely nothing with her, not the smallest bundle. She was only allowed over the frontier because she had a letter from me, saying that we would employ her as a maid in the hotel. The next day, Gennaro went out, bought some underwear and gave it to her to wear in the hotel.

Everyone who has lived in our hotel knows how severe and proud the Italians are: there was never any hint of impropriety. Gennaro's age made Emma respect him. He treated her like a young ignorant sister and taught her everything. And last Christmas, the first Christmas, they agreed to become sweethearts and he had already decided he would not ask for a dowry.

The family had a cabin on a few square yards of mountain earth and not even a spade, not a rope, nor a basket to carry

47

things in; not even a pail. There he spent his holidays. He went down to the nearest village, bought a washtub, a pail, a spade, a fork, a hoe, a basket and some seed; and in spite of the winter weather he showed them how to use the stones he had loosened in the soil to pave part of the floor of their cabin. The stones bruised their bare feet and they had no rags to wrap them in, so he bought one pair of sabots. They agreed to let him marry Emma. He told Emma what had taken place and said to her with our consent:

"I love you and in due time, when we have some savings, I should like to marry you. You are my idea of a good wife and I am quite sure you never looked at another man. Do not answer me at once but think it over for a week. I know I am old and only a man-of-all-work in a small hotel, but if we work hard together we will become something better. It is my duty to see you do not do anything against your wishes, for I am an experienced older man, a city man, and you only a peasant from the mountains."

Emma agreed to this and a year later they were married. Emma had developed and had begun to laugh; she had grown rosier and stouter.

Gennaro was a small man and more talkative than his wife. He took his position as married man and as elder son very seriously. He thought about it too much. Then Gennaro grew jealous. He said Emma should be kept in the laundry and kitchens until she had learned everything; she was so ignorant that she would be embarrassed in public; she ought not to serve in the dining room, the bedrooms were no place for her.

He should have been satisfied. His mother came past every morning. She had much more sense than her son and he listened to her respectfully. She said:

"She's a woman in a thousand, there's not a better woman in the world. Be good to Emma and do what she says."

Then she told me that Gennaro was unfortunate.

"My poor boy's head is not quite right. He was obliged to join the Mussolini youth, he was a Ballilla as a child. I could say nothing. Gennaro is honest and he thinks others are too; he is credulous."

Gennaro would come in happy and refreshed from these morning conversations with his mother; and perhaps from the fresh breeze, the air of the lake, the view of the steep peaks on the French side and the Bernese Oberland and the water rippling.

Emma would be working inside somewhere and he would say

a cheerful word to her, go upstairs to his work, be by her side when she was preparing the vegetables and salads for lunch. After the day's work, Gennaro's spirits fell and sometimes at the servants' meals, which took place in the kitchen one hour before the guests' mealtimes, he would sit pinched, depressed, unable to say a word and eating little. Emma understood him and kept up a cheerful manner, sitting next to him and answering people in a quietly friendly way but always reserved. She took it for granted that her husband would be jealous and tired from his work. It happened that the Mayor one Friday morning was in a gay mood. He sent in Document 191 to say that the coffee was very good, remarkably German, and asked who made it. The answer came back that no one knew. Friday was a quiet day. You would not think perhaps from what I say, how very peaceful the hotel is in that off season just before spring. You could hear a ski boot drop on the attic floor. It was too quiet. The servants began to think of their homes and whether they would lose their jobs if the season continued quiet. Gennaro had time to be jealous. Luisa and Emma went on making things for their linenchests. Mrs. Trollope began to feel her sciatica more. Meanwhile Rosa, the schoolteacher's daughter from Lucerne, had got the star part in a play run by the German-Swiss Catholic Daughters' Association. She stuck her thumb showily in Madame Blaise's soup, she swaggered about the dining room. She was to be found in the street, garden and house shadowed by a tall young German-Swiss, a businessman, who said she was his cousin. Mrs. Trollope met them on the stairs going up to the servants' rooms.

"This is my cousin," said Rosa boldly.

"How do you do?" said Mrs. Trollope politely, but even she noticed their smiles.

Rosa had sold Mrs. Trollope two tickets for the play, which was called *The Dark Spot,* meaning a dark spot in someone's career, and was in dialect. The tickets also had lottery numbers on them. Mrs. Trollope was quite excited about the play, saying Rosa was bold but smart and ambitious. She said:

"I don't understand German and I don't suppose I'll know what it is about."

"If you did understand German you wouldn't know what it is about," said my husband, smiling disagreeably and meaning that no one could understand the dialect in the play but someone like myself.

But Mrs. Trollope asked what color dress Rosa would be

wearing in the last act and she sent her a shoulder-spray to match. Mrs. Trollope did not understand that this kind of thing upsets the servants and makes them jealous. During the two days after that, Mrs. Trollope would call to Luisa as usual when she heard her on the stairs, saying, "My head aches so much, do come and rub it, please, Luisa;" and Luisa, so kindhearted, pretended to be deaf. When she did at last come in, it was with the expression of an angry cat and she said:

"Madame thinks Rosa is very clever, the German young lady is very clever, eh? Like an electric lamp! When she wants to! She pulls it on and off, like a lamp. No doubt she is beautiful too? As beautiful as a dancing bear! And I can imagine how beautifully she would dance the ballet. Beautiful! Bell-is-si-ma!"

Luisa gave a rascally laugh. She was pale and irritable. "The English admire horses also."

She came down to me and said, "She is a very well-born English lady, a little altered in appearance by her residence in the Orient!"

"Luisa! That is forbidden," I said firmly.

"Ah, yes. I am not beautiful and clever. A Catholic daughter indeed. An occasional Catholic daughter, a semi-occasional Catholic daughter."

Mrs. Trollope asked me: "What is the matter with Luisa? She won't come near me and my head is so bad."

I tried to explain about sending the shoulder-spray.

"Ah, Selda, I must love people. It is all that consoles me for living abroad. And you know, my daughters and my son are not writing to me, to punish me, to force my hand. It is not my fault."

I could not stop her calling me Selda. She said I was the same age as her eldest daughter. She had married very young out East.

On the Saturday morning Mrs. Trollope and Madame Blaise set off along the esplanade. Sometimes they walked as far as the crumbled Haldiman Tower, sometimes only as far as the Sandoz monkeys in the public gardens. At other times they went beyond the Tower, round the elbow turn where a clear gutter runs into the lake. The swans dabble there and you can see far up the lake towards the Rhone mouth, the Devil's Horns, the great west wall of the Rhone valley and, above, the first peaks of the Bernese Oberland, rolling on like heavy surf. From there they might turn up to the bus stop just above the school and go into Lausanne, or they would come back again, dawdling from seat to seat.

We tidied up their rooms and I measured Mrs. Trollope's

bedroom. In summer, if busy, we squeeze two beds into her room, and I had just engaged a bedmaker to make two stout but narrow cots which would fit in, one into her room, one into Mr. Wilkins's. If they did not move or double up, I should have to charge them double for the summer season. Mrs. Trollope had noticed the bedmaker working in the backyard and was very pleased.

I put up the menus on both entrances and in the lift. I went into the kitchen at eleven to see that all was going forward. Gennaro was there looking so cross that I did not speak to him. Luisa made a sign to me, followed me out and said rapidly:

"This yellow woman"—meaning Clara "has made trouble. Gennaro has sent Emma to her room and is doing her work. Go and see her please, Signora. It is very bad."

Emma was sitting on her bed sewing. When I came in, she arose and looked me in the face, without concealing her tears. She handed me, without a word, a postcard, a colored postcard, with edelweiss, gentian, the sort of thing you can buy anywhere in Switzerland for twenty-five centimes. It was postmarked Lausanne, dated the day before, and written crabbed, anonymous, as follows:

Who made the worst coffee ever made in this hotel on Friday morning? Emma has other things to think about than coffee. Emma is too much interested in young men to work. What happened the day of the street fair? What happened about ten o'clock this week, Thursday evening, when Emma went upstairs with a strange man she met in Acacia Passage? While Gennaro was helping Charlie to bed? Signed: Some-one who sees and doesn't like hypocrites.

I sent Emma back to the kitchen and made Gennaro come to me in the office.

"Who are you, Gennaro, to change the roster round? It is Emma's turn in the kitchen. We are not pleased with you. You have begun to make trouble, just like some others not to be named. We have been very good to you, helped you to get married, stood by you when the police came about your work permit. We have had an Italian waiter sent back to Italy already because there was not enough work for him. We have not only you, but Luisa, Lina, Clara, Rosa, I don't know how many mouths to feed, more servants than guests in the off season and you spend your spare time making trouble. Emma is not yours to send to her room, she is mine: she is my employee. I shall speak to your mother."

He said: "I am a disgraced man. She has been talking to men. I don't know what to do. She cannot be in the same room as me. It is too much. An honest man can't bear it. They are mocking me."

I told him to go upstairs and help Herman with the floorwaxing. I said, finally:

"Mr. Bonnard will be back shortly and he will talk to you, Gennaro. What you are doing to your wife is very wicked and I doubt if God will forgive you. I know what your mother will say to you."

He went out sulkily. When Roger came back from uptown, I told him. For the first time, Roger had been invited to join a little friendly association of five or six restaurant and hotel proprietors of our sort who felt that prices should be raised a little on the *table d'hôte* meals to raise the tone of the place. It was quite an honor that they should worry about whether we undercut them or not. But with Roger nothing is too small. He is at his best in a crisis; and it is then one understands his success.

If he has been up all night in some cellar drinking with officers in the army and cabaret managers, he will come home green and sorry, but will say:

"The lease on the Venice Café can be called in any day. The man was fool enough to trust the good nature of his landlord; and he is going to find himself without a penny next week and will have to start again as head waiter."

Roger's head is always clear, no matter what his stomach says.

Roger said: "We will stop this before it starts."

At lunchtime the guests were absorbed as usual by the menu and the poor quality of the meal the poor old German cook served them. If they noticed anything it was Clara's wonderful good humor. She was everywhere, chatting with everyone, sweet tempered, willing, her languages were better than usual, she was happy as a child. Only when Luisa put her head with its pointed tongue in the door of the serving hatch and sang like Figaro, *Nu-me-ro quin-di-ci*! did Clara's expression change. "Fünfzehn you mean," she said suddenly in German. I said to Roger, "Look at her."

He frowned. He is a man of stern unprejudiced justice. As soon as everything was cleaned up and the cook had taken himself off, Roger sent for the servants in a body. He shut the office door and took them into the inner room, the sewing room. Then he showed them the anonymous postcard suddenly, told them what it said and remarked:

"One of you wrote it. I don't suppose it was Emma or Gennaro. It is one of you and you had better confess it at once or I shall send for the police. If I find you out and you have not confessed, you will march right out of this hotel without a reference and I will see you get on the police record."

Luisa said at once: "And also it cannot be Charlie. He is in bed with a floating kidney. And it cannot be me. I am not jealous or mad."

"You will go out on the landing and come in one by one. Emma will remain here. Gennaro will go out. Emma! Perhaps you suspect someone?"

Emma gravely shook her head. "If I knew I would tell you."

I said quickly, "I want to tell you that the handwriting is disguised and I think it is a disguised German script and there is a funny mistake in French such as a German might make, I do not think it is any Italian. Now, Emma, who made the coffee on Friday morning?" (That was the morning the Mayor sent me the Document about it. The coffee was bad.)

There was no one there but Gennaro himself, and Clara of course.

They came in one by one but no one confessed. Rosa seemed angry and red, talked about her pride and said she was sorry she had ever left home. I told her the play *A Dark Spot* had gone to her head; she was only a waitress. She tossed her head.

"I am only a waitress, as you put it; but very soon I shall be in a very different situation. I am merely learning the business for my own reasons."

"If you are learning the business, you will learn to get rid at once of anyone writing an anonymous letter. Please let us see your handwriting."

She said: "I'm afraid I'm like yourself, Madame. I don't write very good French."

In the end no one confessed and we had to be satisfied with the idea that Clara had organized the whole thing and had outmaneuvred us. Gennaro and Emma did not speak for nearly two weeks. Rosa left to work in the Hotel Acacias and soon left that to go home. I believe this terrible incident formed

Emma's character, which was always firm. A few days later Gennaro's mother told me Gennaro's soul and mind had been warped by his experience as a child.

"He had not a very active mind and was never able to grasp the ideas which I had and his father had: we were pacifists. I made a mistake and did not think the Italian people would accept Mussolini and then I kept saying he would last only another year or two. Gennaro became a blackshirt when he was nine years old. I could not come back to Switzerland where I was born and he was born and I could not explain anything to him because of the terror. At his school when they were only six or seven the children were asked to name the different kinds of pigs and one child got up to say, My father says that Mussolini is the biggest of the pigs. The Fascists visited his house and the parents were taken away and never seen again. That is why he is like this. I did not belong to the party for years. I kept on asking to come back to Switzerland to work and at last someone said to me, "Join the Fascists and you will get your permit easily." I held out and did not believe it. In the end I joined the Fascists and three months later I got my permit. That is the way Gennaro was brought up—anxious and ignorant; but he is very good."

However, she talked to him about Emma and he forgave his wife.

When Clara's day off came, she said she was sick and stayed in bed. Mrs. Trollope sent up a bottle of vermouth, Clara's favorite drink. The next day Clara was quite yellow and suffering from pains in the stomach. I told Mrs. Trollope Clara was suffering from a guilty conscience and greed; she had probably hoped to marry Gennaro herself. Mrs. Trollope sighed and said:

"Oh, poor Clara: jealousy and loneliness are cruel diseases, it is a sickness. When I am passing the church I shall go in and pray for Clara, for I know what loneliness is. Do you know what she told me, she said, 'I am glad to be sick in bed, it makes me forget my old age when I will be chucked out on the street. There's nothing ahead and no one is going to take care of me.' And she laughed, she didn't cry."

The next Thursday, Clara and I went out on an expedition right after dinner, leaving Luisa to baby-sit. Clara and I were hurrying along, giggling, for we were on a secret mission. We met Mrs. Trollope walking out by herself. Madame Blaise never went out in the evening for fear of catching cold. We explained where we were going, to the Zig-Zag nightclub to look at the photographs of the artists posted outside. I told Mrs. Trollope that when business was quiet Roger was out in town a good deal at night. My best friend Julie, the one who was trying to have an affair with Roger, had been in the day before, smoking, talking and trying to upset me. She said she really was my friend, and to give proof of it she would now tell me that Roger was disgracing himself by going out with a striptease dancer who wore a leopard skin and was now at the Zig-Zag Club. While she was telling me this, she was taking powder from my box, shaking my puff in the air, telling me my makeup was of the wrong color; and she turned and noticed a new photograph of Olivier.

"Since when did Olivier have a twisted nose? Did he fall? He used to be so sweet. He is getting more and more like your family."

I said his nose didn't change: he was probably trying to imitate a rabbit. But I couldn't see anything myself.

"Because her nose is out of joint with jealousy," said Clara.

Mrs. Trollope said: "Come, Selda, we'll all go along and look at the photographs. I don't believe it for a minute."

Then we all three went off laughing. Mrs. Trollope said we would have a drink somewhere and amuse ourselves, "and you will show your friend Julie that you have plenty of friends."

Clara was wearing the new cream-colored suit given to her by Mrs. Trollope. It fitted her wonderfully; she turned round and round under the street lamp lifting her coattails like a duck to show the fit. Mrs. Trollope said:

"Let's have a good time; we won't worry about anything or anyone."

I had left orders with the porter to shut the hotel doors at ten o'clock sharp. The Mayor of B. had been away since early morning, to sell tickets in his lottery. The day before he had spread out all his clothes and all his possessions on the floor and furniture in the two rooms and had pinned numbers to them. He gave duplicate numbers to all the servants and to Roger, Olivier and me. He said he was having a lottery and whoever got the right numbers would get prizes. He had even pinned numbers to what he was wearing. Luisa and I had a fit of laughter which held up the marketing for half an hour, but Rosa said she was afraid of him; Madame Blaise now would not go along the staircase or landings without a flashlight on account of Herman, and Dr. Blaise had spoken roughly to him. Mrs. Trollope stopped laughing:

"I have a haunted feeling; and I dreamed I saw the Mayor standing glowering in a corner of the landing, with his hat, muffler and smoked glasses and his hands out ready to jump on me!"

Tonight I had left orders for the Mayor to be left outside the door until Roger came home, whatever time that was. When Roger came back this afternoon, I told Clara and Mrs. Trollope, I flew at him and told him what Julie said. His pride was hurt. Without a word he went straight out again and did not come back for dinner. The Dutch ladies did not have their wine, and Madame Blaise was angry because she could not have her walnuts. That was because Roger took with him the key of the dessert-cupboard. Mrs. Trollope said:

"Still, it is no use bottling those things up; you see, now you are quite lighthearted. I don't believe your dear husband would ever wrong you."

When we got to the Zig-Zag Club we looked at all the photographs, but the striptease dancer was not among them. Mrs. Trollope said we would go inside and ask; so we all went in laughing. The man at the entrance of course knew me and told us that Wanda the striptease dancer had gone to Geneva a few days before. Mrs. Trollope was delighted.

"Oh, good. Let's celebrate. I feel like a good time."

The man knew Mrs. Trollope too; so he called the manager, who was glad to see us and made us come in to have a drink on the house. Said he:

"We're glad of the company, come along. You'll be my guests. It will make the floor show glad to see some more faces."

"How can they see our faces when their backs are turned?" said Clara, for there was a picture of the floorshow in that position. We were all in the highest spirits.

"What a pity Charlie is not with us; he would make us roar," said Clara.

"Well, what a pity the Mayor is not along, he would buy us a case of champagne," said I.

"The Mayor would make a good floorshow dressed in his smoked glasses," said Clara.

Mrs. Trollope was shocked; but she said:

"Madame Blaise will never forgive me for not moping at

home with her and discussing her great lump of a daughter and her son who looks like a jockey. We shall have a tiff."

At everything we burst out laughing. It was a long time since I had had such a good time. I said:

"It is too good: I am sure something awful will happen. You will see."

"This is quite an adventure," said Mrs. Trollope.

The manager of the Zig-Zag came and sat at our table. He is a man I don't like. He said not to mind about paying. But the question soon came up about our paying for another round of drinks. That is the custom here. Each guest feels obliged to stand treat in his turn. Mrs. Trollope began with:

"I haven't much money with me but I can manage a bottle of champagne."

After that, I was obliged to too; and that is how I got into debt at the Zig-Zag that evening. The manager brought along some people, a jeweler in Lausanne, a café owner. He stood the whole table to champagne, they reciprocated and so it went. In the end we all were tipsy and I owed for one bottle of champagne. But no one regretted it. Mrs. Trollope said:

"This is more like old times. In the East we had never a dull moment. This place is like heaven on a sunny morning but it is rather quiet."

"My father always said heaven would be a bore," said I.

"Drink, fall on you face and be merry, for tomorrow you die," said Clara.

It is a long walk down to the lake shore from Lausanne center. The air gets richer and richer till it is almost like a fish stew. Clara said there were wild boars which come down because of the cold and they would get us. I said we would catch one and take him home for the kitchen. We had to keep stopping for breath and to giggle, but in the end we got home. We got in about two o'clock and found Charlie in his dressing gown and pajamas dozing on the couch in the sitting room. He came at length to the door.

"Bad little girls," he said grinning sourly.

"Is everyone home, Charlie?" said I.

He answered gaily, "Mr. Bonnard is not home. The Mayor of B. is now filling a long-felt want in the lunatic asylum."

"Charlie, don't clown so much."

We were all breathless with the descent, dizzy too; and dizzier still when we heard.

It seems that just after midnight there was a rattling at the front door. Gennaro ran upstairs and looked out from the second floor, so that he could see under the glass awning that fans out over the door. There was the Mayor entirely naked, except for his hat and muffler, but with his two shopping bags. Gennaro wanted to open up quickly, for he thought the Mayor would catch cold. "Supposing some ladies came along," said Charlie. "I'm not strong enough to deal with a circus number like that."

He told Gennaro to phone the police, though they would probably be angry at being called on such a calm cold night. Gennaro telephoned the police, but before they arrived the Mayor had gone. He ran to the Hotel Royal where he got inside the door before the night clerk, who was stretched out on a lounge in the sitting room, knew what was happening.

He asked for a room, said something rude about us, the Hotel Swiss-Touring. The clerk, who had taken refuge behind the desk, was shouting:

"No, no, we have no rooms, the hotel is full up, sir."

But the Mayor yelled:

"It's the off season, you haven't three wretched sinners in the whole mausoleum, there are five miles of corridor occupied by ghosts of dead bankrupt Englishmen in this damp mausoleum; that is all."

You know, they expected no one but a rajah doing the nightclubs, and the night clerk, only a schoolboy, was limp with fear. The Mayor took himself up in the lift, quite naked of course, except for his top piece and neck piece with his two shopping bags, while the boy was saying:

"But, sir, you have no luggage."

The Mayor ran up and down the corridors and then there was a crash. He had taken a chair and was beating one of the mirror-doors leading into an upstairs sitting room. In the dim light of the corridor he had seen a strange naked man advancing upon him and had rushed at him with a plush-and-gilt chair.

Meantime, the clerk had telephoned the police, but the available men were now at our hotel, looking for the Mayor. The boy came running out of the hotel for help, fell in the snow, found the police and very soon they had got the Mayor and delivered him, a pretty little package, to a local institution. The reception office made no trouble about admitting him and there he was.

Mrs. Trollope said: "Oh, poor man. I told you, Selda, he was ready to jump on any one of us!"

"Did you know Mrs. Trollope said he was mad?" I said to Charlie.

Charlie winked. "And now, ladies, go and get some shut-eye."

"Wait till Mr. Wilkins hears what fun and excitement we had. He thinks I am moping here all alone," said Mrs. Trollope.

"Wait till Mr. Bonnard hears that we paid twenty-five francs a bottle for champagne in the Zig-Zag when it is only eleven francs fifty in the Hoirs. I shall have to send the money over in the morning."

Charlie said: "Now that the Mayor is gone, Christmas is over: no more free bubbly."

Roger did not return till seven in the morning. He said nothing to me, looked at Olivier, went down to the basement to see to the furnace. He and Clara were very sick all day; but these mountain people are wiry. When Roger heard about the champagne, he took fifty francs from the safe and went uptown to pay the manager of the Zig-Zag.

As for the Mayor: his relatives came with a lawyer ten days later and it turned out to be a very sad case. He had a wife and three grown children who had to be kept in ignorance of his condition. They put the Mayor on a train to take him back to Belgium; but the way to Belgium is through France; and the French law is that no one can be committed as insane or kept in custody without being committed by a French court and French alienists. The Mayor was always very bright. He knew this and he stepped off the train at the very first stop the express made in France. Perhaps he is still having a good time.

"I think I'll go and find him and join him," Charlie said.

I now had two more rooms vacant and it was then that I took back Miss Chillard, who was coming from Zermatt. She owed us money and had left some of her luggage with us as security; I did not give her her old room, a large double room, but a small one, Number 27.

Mr. Wilkins had been away for a few days, in Paris where he had to meet an old acquaintance from Singapore. When he returned, the cousins met with the joy and effusion of lovers and married people. Then things went on as before.

It was an afternoon. The hotel guests were walking or resting. Mr. Wilkins as usual was stretched out on a lounge chair in the sun, before his open window in his little room; and through the communicating door he could talk to Mrs. Trollope, who was on her bed, with several cushions underneath her head and her hips. She had spread out on her windowsill several handfuls of white breadcrumbs that she had made from the white bread she brought up from lunch. She kept the windows open, the curtains apart, and had made a trail of crumbs from the windowsill across the carpeted floor to several chairs upon which she had trained the sparrows to sit. These chairs were on a wedge-shaped step, a sort of dais, in front of the windows. She lay on her bed with her black curly head raised, waiting. With her black wide eyes, black rimmed as if lined with makeup, she watched the fat sparrows look, call, hesitate, hop, enter and fly as far as the edge of the little dais; and so to the chairs. She was careful not to make a movement, though her neck was aching. They knew she was there and kept looking up at her, as they pecked; but they made a busy sweet sound, "Veet, veet, veet," which she liked. "It means food," she said to Robert. About four o'clock, Robert called out to her:

"Lilia, there is a knocking on my wall."

"Oh, that must be that poor thing, Miss Chillard. I saw a lot of her while you were away and I promised to go in at teatime. You know I meant to take her some cakes."

Mrs. Trollope rose cautiously, but the sparrows flew. She slipped on her shoes, tidied her hair and went out of the hotel. About a hundred yards down the street was a cake shop patronized by herself and Madame Blaise. There she now bought one hundred grams of dry biscuits, just what Miss Chillard had asked for, and a hundred grams of chocolate biscuits, such as Mr. Wilkins liked to have before dinner with his rum and vermouth. When she returned, he said to her:

"Lilia, do make haste and see what that woman wants. She has been knocking on my wall for half an hour. I think she expected me to go in; but I'm blessed if I will and I told her that. I called out, I can't come in, Miss Chillard; I'm a man and I'm in my underwear."

"Robert, the poor thing is in bed; and you have been away—she thought it was I."

"I wish I could believe it."

"I am not staying here to listen to your jokes in bad taste."

"No one listens to jokes in good taste."

"I cannot laugh at your jokes, Robert."

He said calmly: "No wonder everyone takes us for husband and wife."

"To that, Robert, I am not going to say anything. You know only too well what I think and you are trying to provoke me for your own amusement."

"Wake me up about five-thirty, Lilia. We'll have our drink; and don't invite that woman."

"Oh, poor woman. She makes my heart bleed."

"She would probably rather make your bankbook bleed."

"Robert, she is a descendant of William the Fourth, she says."

"Did he leave her enough to live on?"

"She didn't discuss it with me."

"Then he didn't. Be careful, Lilia. Don't commit us. I shall give her nothing and I shall not allow you to give her anything."

"Your years in business, Robert, made you hard-hearted."

But Lilia smiled slightly as she knocked at the door of Number 27. She was grave and sympathetic as she looked at the woman in the bed.

She had seen her, though not known her, on her previous visit. At that time Miss Chillard had been with an older woman, very humble in manner, respectable, whom Mrs. Trollope had taken for a paid companion or poor toady. No one knew her name; she was never introduced. She came down to dinner as soon as the bell rang, ate her soup and then would wait, with her head bowed, for Miss Chillard. If Miss Chillard did not appear, she was nervous, shamefaced, and on one or two nights in succession went up to their room to fetch her companion. Miss Chillard, brought in like this, remained distant, spoke only in a cold peremptory and complaining way to the servants; at the table there was a miserable silence. For a few nights after this the poor relative or aged traveling companion ate her soup, her meat dish and her dessert with hearty appetite alone and would look friendly at the other diners. If Miss Chillard came down for dessert, again she shrank and the silence followed. Miss Chillard rarely ate soup, had special dishes of eggs or vegetables, and took few sweet things. She often finished this slight meal earlier than her companion, when she would sit with an air of rebuke. When she spoke to her friend, it was to say, in her high-bred insulting voice, something like this:

"Perhaps, thinking it over, you had better go back. You can do nothing for me. I shall try to get a position *au pair* to pay my expenses. I'm sure I don't want you wasting any more money or time here."

Though tall and well built, Miss Chillard was underweight and her shoulders deeply bowed. She had certificates from doctors in England and Switzerland that she was always sending home, that is to England, to prove to the Bank of England that it was necessary for her to stay abroad. And it was at this moment, when funds were low, that she must have heard Mrs. Trollope and Mr. Wilkins speaking of money. Mrs. Trollope under a capital export scheme was gradually getting her money out of England. A considerable part of her fortune was in England; but as she had agreed to live abroad for the rest of her life the Bank of England was permitting her gradually to transfer her funds.

Miss Chillard spoke to Mrs. Trollope only after her companion had left for England; and it then turned out that her poor humble companion was her mother. Miss Chillard, the only unmarried daughter of four, a girl with brilliant chances, educated in Switzerland, had had to work on her mother's farm during the war, had had an accident, hurt her back, become a permanent invalid. The British authorities held that she did not need Switzerland, that she would do well enough on the farm in Devonshire.

Two days after her mother left, Miss Chillard took the train for Zermatt, owing us rent and board for both for two months. But she had showed us letters saying that money was on the way from her mother and we had let her go.

But now, after three months, she was back. The Bank of England had turned down all of her numerous applications. Sick as she was and necessary as the mountain air was to her, she must go back to England, where the air poisoned her she said, and where she would die. I myself was touched.

Mrs. Trollope had been sorry for her; now she was startled by the terrible change. In the sagging bed, propped up by pillows, lay a tanned bony church-door martyr, with large bright blue eyes in deep hollows. Her lank hair trailed over the pillows; a loose nightgown with a handsome lace décolletage showed her emaciated neck, bony chest, the wide-set weakened breasts. But the neck had been a column, the chest once broad, deep and strong: there was still determination in this disorder, a high-spirited selfish temper.

Lilia was distressed.

"Oh, dear Miss Chillard, how are you? You don't seem well. Have you seen a doctor?"

Miss Chillard said she had seen two. Mr. Bonnard had sent for one and some dear dear friends in Vevey, who were devoted to her, had sent another: "They are people who would do anything for me. They are moving heaven and earth to get the British Consul to come and see me, so that he will send in a report favorable to my case."

But she was worried, for she must pay the doctors, this she must do first of all; doctors must always be paid. Her mother had gone home to talk to the Bank; she had received no money from the Bank, the Bank had stopped the money she was relying on to pay her debts here and at Zermatt and she did not even know how she was to get home.

Why did the people at home put up with such a stupid government?

What could you expect from the sons of bricklayers and boot menders? If there was a change of government, she was sure her friends would be able to help her, get funds out.

She had stopped here in this wretched hotel, on her way home where she now must go, but she would probably die in this rented room, and in rags, because she had left the rest of her luggage at Zermatt as security. The Bank said she could go to mountains in Great Britain, places quite useless to her. They were dragging her back home to die, because the Labor Government did not understand people like her and did not care for her sort. She was half dead now. She had many friends here; hotel keepers who knew her, respected her, they really adored her and understood her troubles, but she had been obliged to leave them too, friends, hotel keepers and servants alike, without paying anything, having only the little money left she kept for doctors.

"I am worried about you, dear Miss Chillard."

"Do not worry about me, Mrs. Collop. I expect another doctor soon. Dear Madame Blaise is sending me one. Her husband is a doctor and they have friends here. People are always so good to me. But there is someone next door who takes no notice when I knock. It seems strange. I might be very ill."

"Oh, that is my cousin Mr. Wilkins. He is rather shy with women."

It seemed to Mrs. Trollope that Miss Chillard gave her rather a strange glance, cool and amused. Mrs. Trollope blushed.

The invalid lay silent in her bed and her gaze wandered. Her two or three valises stood about on chairs, unlocked. She asked Mrs. Trollope to get her several things from them, a teapot, packets of tea and sugar, some talc and perfume. She spoke clearly and shortly, Lilia found everything at once and did not rummage; yet Miss Chillard seemed restless, mocking. Lilia thought, Oh, poor dear, how poor she is; and she thought she would explain to Mr. Wilkins what it was to be chased out of one hotel after another, a helpless invalid, unable to pay and yet rich enough at home, one of the miseries of these complicated days, the rich turned tramp and beggar.

"Just as I was myself, Robert, till my first money came through: you never realized that that was the first reason I acted as companion to that sick old woman in Vevey—I did not want to ask you for money to pay my expenses."

She had puffed away on those endless walks along the lake behind the invalid chair, thickset, heavy, on her pretty high heels; and she had been treated as helpers are always treated by rich invalids. She said now to Miss Chillard:

"Won't your dear mother be glad to see you? Won't it be better for you, after all, on your lovely farm in Devon, having good country food, better than eating this wretched hotel diet. You don't even eat: you don't take as much as my sparrows that come in every day to eat. Now tell me what you have had to eat today?"

Then Miss Chillard mentioned such a poor diet, things that had been brought and taken away untouched, that Lilia felt miserable and asked Miss Chillard if she could not make her tea.

"Oh, no, thank you, thank you so much, oh, no, I shall manage; you are so sweet," said the woman in her high sweet boarding-school manner.

"Well, can't I get you anything?" said Lilia, oppressed by what she saw. The afternoon sun, hot, brilliant even at this season, poured at the window but not through the window, which was tightly closed, the heavy winter curtains half drawn. It was already sunset in the room. Miss Chillard replied:

"Oh, nothing, thank you—but there is something if you would be so generous, just get me two ounces of water biscuits, I saw them once before when I was here, rather sweet without any flavoring, or just a mild one. I know the name. I shall look for it in my notebook and tell you. I shall make my tea and that is all I really want; and if you would get me my medicine. My purse is in the corner of the green valise, just there in the corner," she ended sharply as Mrs. Trollope lifted the lid of the green valise.

"Oh, but dear Miss Chillard, I brought you some dry biscuits, the sort you said you liked."

"Oh, how good of you, oh, how lovely of you. But I cannot really eat. I shall keep them for the servant, Luisa, as I have really nothing to pay her with and I expect she will be glad of something to eat."

After a few more words, Lilia left Miss Chillard, went to her room and spoke to Mr. Wilkins through the open door, waking him up. There she detailed to him the condition of Miss Chillard and her idea of getting a third doctor.

"But of course, Robert, I am not sure she would not be a world better if she ate some soup and had a little sun. She has half a balcony. I think it very nice of Mr. and Mrs. Bonnard to give her that balcony room when she is in debt to them. The biscuits should have been water biscuits: I made a mistake."

"Well, get her a few and see if she can digest them before you buy half a pound of the things," said Mr. Wilkins.

"Robert, there is one thing about you that comes out and that is your country origin, that grasping farmer strain. One must not look at every penny. When a poor Englishwoman is here and cannot eat anything, there is no harm in making her feel a little happier."

"Get her her medicine and get her one hundred grams of biscuits. She won't eat them. This is a come-on, you'll see: she is leading up to a loan. Buy the biscuits if you must play the Good Samaritan."

"You know I must have something to do, Robert. The thing about our lives now, living abroad, retired, is that I am completely useless. I would rather go and help them peel vegetables in the kitchen. I'll ask Mrs. Bonnard."

"Oh, I'd rather you went and bought Miss Chillard a few biscuits every day. But she is leading up to a touch. I know you'd give away your last shilling and it's a good thing I'm here to see you do not."

A little flushed, Mrs. Trollope again went up the street, to get the medicine and the water-biscuits. When she returned, she was surprised and embarrassed to find two strangers in Miss Chillard's room, a French couple who were trying to speak English. They were poor tourists. The woman, in a black toque

65

and gray suit, was offering a small bottle of liniment to Miss Chillard, and Miss Chillard was explaining in English, though she spoke French, that she needed Vitamin A and not liniment:

"My fingers are so cold; I wish you had brought that instead."

She turned to Lilia, coldly: "They don't seem to understand. Would you tell her that, Mrs. Collop? But don't refuse the liniment, take the liniment, I don't want to hurt her feelings. Put it on the glass shelf above the basin, with the other bottles, where I can get it. I shall ask the Italian maid to rub me. Perhaps I shall get some feeling back into my legs and arms;" and she said to the French couple:

"My maid will rub me with it."

They at once looked at Mrs. Trollope and drew together a bit.

The French husband, in a shop-made striped suit and pointed shoes, with a thin harassed face, had brought Miss Chillard some chocolates, an offering which he had shyly put out of the way on the table, for he could see it was not appropriate to her grand manner. The French couple looked at Lilia with such reticence that Lilia felt she was intruding. Perhaps there was a secret between the three. She excused herself after putting the water-biscuits on a bedside table and saying:

"I should be glad to make tea for you."

"Oh, no, thank you. I am trying to explain to them what I want but they don't understand. I met them at Zermatt and they were very good to me. They are generous creatures, but they don't know what I want."

The French couple were saying: "Oh, but you must eat; pills are a poor substitute for food."

There had been no introduction and Mrs. Trollope knew she was taken for a maid, a common trick of genteel women down on their luck. Sometimes Madame Blaise tried it on, when they were shopping in Lausanne, making out that Mrs. Trollope was a professional guide or shopper: once Mrs. Trollope had been offered a buyer's percentage.

Shortly after, she heard the French couple on the landing. She looked out with the idea of asking them a question; but as they stood dubiously and dowdily side by side, deploring something, and as they huddled together when they saw her, she withdrew.

After a time she went back and said to Miss Chillard, who

was lying flat on her back staring in front of her:

"You know, our rooms are next to yours. Just knock if you feel faint in the night and I will come."

"Oh, thank you so much; oh, I think I would rather rouse the night watchman than you."

"Oh, no. That's Charlie. You know he is also the porter and is ill. He sleeps on the couch in the parlor. He needs sleep. He should be in hospital. Please call me. My husband's room is next to yours."

"Yes, I know, thank you," said Miss Chillard, still staring in front of her. Mrs. Trollope was unhappy. She did not like to say Mr. Wilkins was her husband, but she did not like to tell her story immediately to a stranger, and she felt ashamed of herself with unmarried women: she thought they suffered so much. But Miss Chillard, a roomer in hotels, pensions and friends' houses since a child, might understand?

When they were having their rum, she said to Mr. Wilkins:

"We are English; shouldn't we do something about poor Miss Chillard?"

"Why? She has survived to the age of thirty-five without us."

"But it is different now. And I feel for the honor of the English on the Continent. It is the unpaid bills."

"Frankly, Lilia, what honor do you think the English have ever had on the Continent?"

"That's a strange thing to say."

"The English have always been mocked as unreliable, awkward, ignorant, provincial and poor."

"Robert, it is the Scot in you that says that."

He said nothing.

"If she knocks in the night, let me know."

"I shall probably not hear a sound."

"I am afraid she is really ill, though."

"If she dies, what difference will it make to you, Lilia?"

"You make friends so easily, Robert. People remark about your charm and ease of manner. They do not see you as you really are."

"Let's go and rest. Tomorrow we have this dinner with the Blaises."

"And, Robert, we must take out this man who is trying to sell you a car; we must take out the Pallintosts."

Wilkins said: "Yes. Well, I have invited them for tomorrow evening too. It is my party. I drew out a bit more money than I expected. I think it a bit stiff that when they are here to sell me a car I should have to take them out as well, but I shall take it off his commission, Pallintost's I mean."

Lilia went into her room and shut the door. Immediately, she heard a knocking on her wall; it was Madame Blaise's signal. Lilia looked haggard. She opened the intervening door and went in to Madame Blaise. Madame Blaise addressed her in a society voice,

"Liliali, what have you been doing? Come and arrange my hair for me." Madame Blaise seated herself before the wooden table on which was a large square mirror in a silver frame, brought from her house in Basel. She had spread out her toilet articles, which were to match in heavy silver. She handed the brush to Lilia, saying:

"Hair first; and then we can try another makeup."

Madame Blaise was a tall heavy woman of German type, with blue eyes and white hair. Mrs. Trollope set to work. It was a long job. They tried the thick straight hair this way and that. In the meantime Doctor Blaise, a brisk, elderly but dark-haired man with an amused smile, kept coming in through the door leading to his double room at the corner of the building which was kept for him on his weekends. The Blaises had a villa on the other side of Switzerland, four hours away by train, where Dr. Blaise had his practice; but he was so well known that he visited patients here too. Doctor Blaise teased the two beauties, as he called them.

At five-thirty they passed through the two doors into Mr. Wilkins's room, where they had rum, sugar, water, lime juice and after that a vermouth chaser, Robert's own recipe. Afterwards, Madame Blaise returned to her room, put on her outdoor clothes, and went down with them to dinner in the dining room.

In the morning early, Robert looked in at her door and said the woman next to him was rapping on the wall again—"The woman's a blessed poltergeist!"—and at this very moment, Madame Blaise, hearing them, started rapping on her wall:

"Liliali, Liliali, come and talk to me!"

Mrs. Trollope sighed, groaned:

"Oh, my heart beat all night to suffocate me and now I must talk to these women."

"Well, I am sure I am not going into either of them in my dressing gown," said Robert leaving his door open and going back to bed with the morning newspapers, where he had begun to draw his charts and graphs of market values.

Mrs. Trollope rose, brushed her hair. She wore an old-fashioned high-necked pink flannel nightgown with cuffs and collar scalloped in silk, the sort of thing she had worn as a girl in the convent. She put on her striped flannel dressing gown and went in to see Miss Chillard.

"Oh, dear Mrs. Collop, I had such a wretched night without sleep, but I would not call you, as that man is not very responsive. I wonder if you would mind putting out my tea things? I cannot bear the tea they send up to me."

"I sympathize, their tea is awful. I have got into the habit of going down and getting my own hot water. But Madame Bonnard takes it personally and says I must send for the servants, that is what they are here for. But if you like I shall go down just the same and get you some really hot water."

"Oh, how very kind, but I think I shall wait for the girl, the servant. Would you mind finding me the shetland bed jacket? I am afraid I am a little décolletée in this nightgown and the doctor is coming."

The same thing occurred. While Mrs. Trollope was going through the brown valise, though she carefully followed directions she felt she was being watched. She thought again there must be money in the valises. She flushed.

"Oh, thank you very much, thank you so much. I am afraid it does not really help."

"Don't you think you should get some fresh air? It's a lovely morning."

"With my trouble, I can never trust to the air. Perhaps, later on. I have friends in Vevey; they adore me and they may come to take me out. But I am so weak—Mrs. Scallop—and I cannot eat anything. I got up last night, fell on the floor from weakness and spent the night on the floor. I am dirty on one side but I am not strong enough to wash."

Mrs. Trollope offered to wash her, gave her advice. Miss Chillard could not do any of the things suggested.

As Mrs. Trollope went on talking, the two women looked at each other speculatively. There was a faint supercilious smile in Miss Chillard's wasted face; perhaps she did not know this. She must have been a real beauty, thought Mrs. Trollope. How these English stay-at-home girls wasted their lives. She must have been a spoiled child, the beauty of the family, something had turned her into a hypochondriac. Perhaps she had had a lover and was suffering from that lingering and languishing disease. Lilia formed all kinds of ideas about the sick woman, as she saw her in the bright morning light reflected from the lake.

Miss Chillard watched the sunburnt, weathered woman with a bright still look, and her smile deepened. Mrs. Trollope knew very well what she was thinking. This woman is a Eurasian, that is why the man won't marry her.

As she talked to her about the sagging mattress, the winter curtains which should now be changed for summer weight, about the insufficient heating and that Miss Chillard should ask for an electric heater for windy evenings, she thought that perhaps Miss Chillard's illness was self-induced: she was a brave malingerer-errant who was not afraid of homelessness but of home, and who knew enough about people to cast herself on the mercy of hotel keepers, of casual acquaintances; and could not bear those at home who knew her sadness. Who would lead such a life? "And I am leading it," said Mrs. Trollope to herself.

Miss Chillard was saying:

"Oh, I have cheated hotel keepers before this, but I can't feel myself responsible. You see, I am so unwilling to go out of Switzerland, because I am afraid they won't let me in again. I am rather a suspect." She moved her handsome shoulders and smiled her luminous smile. She continued:

"My brother-in-law was here a few days ago but I refused to go back with him. It would be quite wrong. They think he can influence me; but they are quite wrong. I knew him long ago before he married my sister. One must be careful in a family. I told him to go back. Something may happen. I have showered the Bank of England with doctors' certificates and one always hopes they will take some notice. But as far as I can see the Bank is merely enriching the Swiss doctors and impoverishing the Swiss hotel keepers. There seems to be no logic in anything they do; but I suppose they bow the knee to the Labor Government."

Mrs. Trollope said: "Oh, naturally, we are all miserable with the Labor Government. I have never lived long in England and the idea of going there now makes me wretched, and yet I so long to be among my own, among people who speak English all their lives, even though their England isn't England to me. But it is home. I have children there, I am afraid if I am away so long they will become strangers to me."

Mrs. Trollope said she must look for her letters and she went.

After she and Mr. Wilkins had eaten their breakfast, they put on their outdoor clothes and were to be seen picking their way across that part of the esplanade which is near the Nautical Club. This part was now being repaved; and one large and one small Walo-Bertschinger roller-tractor were running over and over the new tarring. They called them the Walo Dragons or the Walos; and each day they went to observe them.

"It amuses me; I am glad there is something to look at," said Mr. Wilkins.

Mrs. Trollope said: "About Miss Chillard: do you know, Robert, I felt uneasy. I don't like the name of England being dragged down by these people. I am ashamed to say it, for I expect she is really sick, but I am haunted by the idea that she is a bit of a fraud."

Mr. Wilkins said: "I shouldn't worry about that, Lilia. You know we always pay our bills; and in fact Mrs. Bonnard knows that at this moment we have in their safe over a thousand Swiss francs."

Mrs. Trollope still nervous, said she did not see the sense of this either. For one thing the money was partly hers yet it was there in his name.

"Supposing you went to Geneva or Basel about this motorcar the Pallintosts want to sell us and I suddenly needed money, Mr. Bonnard would be quite within his rights if he refused it to me. He is so scrupulous. My name should be on it too."

What emergency could possibly arise? You have your money with mine in the bank. You know, Lilia, we must be careful; we are living abroad; we have not yet decided what we are going to do."

"What is there in living abroad? I am so unhappy."

"What a funny day, Lilia. Sun, wind, rain and clouds."

"Yes, Mr. Blot the taximan says it is marrying weather. They have a proverb here, marry on a day with four weathers, then the marriage will weather all changes. I wish we could get married here, Robert. I see no sense in our remaining this way. It is absurd a man your age being tied to an old mother and three sisters, maiden ladies in their fifties and sixties. Why, you scarcely knew them. And you don't like them. I send them Christmas cards; you don't. And they know all about us but they pretend not to. Your family is full of hypocrisy."

"I promised my mother not to marry during her lifetime; and I won't."

"But, Robert, she is blind, deaf and partly paralyzed. She has lost her memory. And you don't believe in a personal God."

"Just the same, she does; and I swore on her Bible; and she is still alive."

"Do you think it was right of your mother to make her children promise not to marry? Look at your sisters now! Wasted lives!"

"You see, Lilia, that is not the question. The question is, Did they promise? And they did."

"It's wrong to get a promise from girls who don't know what they're talking about."

"Chrissie and Cathy were in their mid-twenties and it has made no difference to me." He had a soft tranquil laugh, which she now heard.

"It makes a difference to me. My daughters and my son are very unhappy about the way I am living."

"You forget, Lilia, that they are Mr. Trollope's children. Their feelings would not affect my mother or sisters. And then, would it be right? He gave each of them a settlement when you divorced; he did not mean them to be mine."

"Oh, Robert, you are so starched. You don't belong to this world."

"On the contrary, I believe I am acquainted with the ways of this world; and I think I have managed our little affairs very well the last twenty-five years. We have brought up your children and spent our lives together and not a soul the wiser, or none cares to mention it. I am known throughout the rubber world as an exemplary bachelor."

"If you are so exemplary, why don't you marry me? Your mother need never know. We are living abroad."

"My dear Lilia, I never promised to marry you; I do not like I.O.U's. I did not know when I would be able to. When mother passes on it will be time enough for us to think about this question."

"If there were some money to come to you, I might understand better," said Lilia.

Mr. Wilkins laughed frankly. "Oh, perhaps the old girl is hanging on in the hopes of inheriting from me. I control all the money in the family but my married sister Margaret's. But I fancy I shall disappoint mother."

Lilia turned away and wrung her hands in the little

72

handkerchief which she had just taken out of her bag.

"Oh, if I could only say what I feel—"

"Do not try, Lilia; or you will be as troublesome as usual."

Lilia cried: "Oh, what is the use of money when it is no use? Our money is shut up and we are in jail because we must stay with it. Here I am living abroad. You want me to bring out all my money; I will have none there. I won't be able to go and see my girls for Christmas unless they take me in. And I'm a rich woman. This system of money has nothing to do with my life. What is the use of so much calculation? We live in the cheapest hotel in town. Suppose you live on till ninety-three, because your family does that, it is long-lived, and we go to Nice or Davos or Zermatt or Casablanca or the Argentine, all places I don't like and where I don't feel at home, just because it is good for our money? But that means the money has us. I tell you I wish you were not so efficient, Robert, and that I had some free money. And then, if you allow me to buy something, it is a jeweled movement or a diamond ring which are really investments. I am ashamed of Miss Chillard but in a sense it is true: it is the Bank makes her a cheat; and you are my bank."

Robert said indulgently: "Lilia, you are a child and always will be. Just leave these little problems to me. I am accustomed to them and can handle all that for you. That is one of my functions in your life."

Lilia said, with a rain and mist of tears in her black eyes and on her face tanned and dried by many oriental suns:

"But I want to be free. Life seems very small to me this way. And what are Mme. Bonnard and Mme. Blaise? Are they my old friends? Are they the kind of people I would pick out for myself? They are very nice but I can't go on all my life trying to love people at the *table d'hôte*. Even the U.S.A. would be better."

Robert said composedly:

"Do you remember that man on the S.S. *Jaffa*? You know, the one they called the P.M.'s right eye and he had only one eye—a left eye, incidentally? Do you know that fellow said that Mme. Chiang Kai-shek and the other sisters—Soong, is it?—sent all their money back to the U.S.A. The Americans gave it to them and the Americans might have kept it. But all they did was hand it over and stamp it Soong. But I think the sisters made a mistake. The yankee dollar is supporting too many countries and adventures; this is mere ABC whatever Madame Blaise thinks. She is only worried about the money she salted away there on trust; but in her name. She's quite an interesting customer. So is he. But they're not getting their trademark on any of our money, incidentally. Everyone around you, Lilia, sees that you are gullible."

He went on for a long time and Lilia said her head was aching; she had not slept the night before, and his idea about recalling facts and names had been useless again to genuine insomnia: the facts and names had kept her awake.

"Very well, Lilia, but it is your own fault. Two good plates of soup at lunch and dinner would send you to sleep."

Mrs. Trollope went upstairs and threw herself on the bed; but she left the door ajar and when she saw Luisa, she called her feebly through the door.

"Luisa, Luisa, j'ai mal à la tête, venez, s'il vous plaît."

Yesterday she had offended Luisa again by talking about Rosa.

"I saw Rosa out walking Sunday with her beau and she looked so happy, she was quite pretty, bella, Luisa."

Luisa with a "bell-l-la" had looked long at Mrs. Trollope in an icy passion of jealousy. Half an hour later she made an opportunity to come into the room, and walking up to the photograph of Mrs. Trollope's eighteen-year-old daughter, Madeleine, a ravishing brunette, and pointing to it, she said:

"Sua figlia è bella: sua figlia bell-l-liss-sima! Mais cette fille est rouge et noire comme une poupée! Capisce, Madama, Madama capisce? Paint, molto, molto, rouge et noir. Non è bella; brutta, brutta!"

And then, after a short cold silence, Luisa had shown a set of fascinating wiles, delightful smiles, half words in English, soothing and loving. Luisa could be angry, acid, contemptuous. She had flying passions, transparent guile: she was fluid, clever and really affectionate. She responded to every advance. Sometimes Mrs. Trollope spoke to her as to a daughter. She came in now.

"Buon giorno, Signora. Come sta? Sta male? Povera donna!"

Mrs. Trollope said, "Si, si, male, Luisa. Please rub the back of my neck."

She raised herself and Luisa rubbed her thin strong hands in a certain way over Mrs. Trollope's neck and shoulders. As she did it, they talked in their way.

"I cannot stay long now, Madame, because I have all the next floor to do. Someone left and I must turn out the room. Another guest will be here at five o'clock."

"Oh, you must not leave me. You must try to come back tonight."

Presently Mrs. Trollope said: "Oh, what a shame it is, Luisa, that I cannot go out and enjoy this lovely day and you, too."

"I don't see that it is so nice. The sun goes down early behind the mountain range and there is always snow on the hills. They stick up like combs," said Luisa nastily.

"I think it is sad, molto triste, Luisa, that you can see your fiancé only once a year."

Luisa said quickly, in the mixture of tongues that they spoke: "You know, Signora, you say it is lovely here, but winter comes and I only love spring, primavera. Yes, the days are lovely in spring. I don't mind getting up at six. It is light. The sky is clear and the water is often quite blue. I can go swimming. There are flowers everywhere. I don't even mind the summer very much, though we work from morning to night and of course we don't then get the rest we are supposed to have, in the afternoon. But I don't like the autumn or winter. I can't love them. Spring, don't you think, is youth, beauty, it is everything! Here things look pretty—but it is dead. I come from Lago di Garda. You would think the water was covered with white daisies in the morning in spring with the light floating; and at night the stars make thousands of little lights in the water. What is there here to compare with that?"

"I heard you singing in Miss Chillard's room this morning."

"I sing a little but I do not feel like singing. I sing so that she will feel better. Don't you go to see the poor English lady?"

"Oh, I do go and everyone goes, Luisa. I don't know what she is going to do. She says she can't pay you anything, you know."

Luisa said angrily: "I don't care about that. If she is sick, I try to cheer her up. I think once she was beautiful; don't you think so? But so thin now—ai-ai-ai!—it's hard to look straight at her. It's a pity she didn't marry an Englishman when she was a girl. I think she was disappointed and then she decided to become ill. I think that man who came to see her was the man."

"Which man? Her brother-in-law?"

"Fratello—no!" said Luisa somberly.

"Eh? In-law?"

"Law—legge!"

"Ah!"

After thinking it over, she said, "No capisco," sulkily.

"You mean, she kissed him—kiss?" Mrs. Trollope acted out a kiss.

"No, no! She sent him away. She en colère—angery. She say: 'Go a-way! I not wish see you.' He say: 'Siamo amici, we are friends, surely.' She say: 'I ave no friends. Solamente uno in Zermatt. In Zermatt one'—I think e is il dottore. Si."

"The doctor?"

Luisa said rapidly: "Perché, she say: 'Just elp me to go to my doctor, in Zermatt; I wish nothing more.'"

But Mrs. Trollope said: "But that is her doctor she had to leave because she could not pay."

"No, no, I know; I see, I ear. I know," said the perceptive Luisa. "I was counting laundry, out in the all."

"And so you think he was the one? The brother-in-law?"

"Of course. That is why they sent im."

"Luisa, ask Madame Bonnard to let me help you with the rooms. If I could work I wouldn't have these headaches. A man can waste his time and read books but a woman is useful."

"Ah, poor Madame," said Luisa moodily.

Luisa arranged a few things and then said: "I must go. Now you must get up and get ready to eat or you will feel sick, like the other day. And I think you should go and see the poor English lady—is she a signora or a signorina?"

"A signorina."

"Yes; I thought so. She must go home and marry an Englishman."

At lunch Robert was still reading his morning paper. She said:

"I beg you, Robert, do not read the paper in my face! What will people think? They will say, What a rude man! I am not used to this."

"Please let me finish this article, Lilia."

The habit had grown upon him fast, suddenly, indeed in the past few months. He had not done it when he first came. Mrs. Trollope rose and went to Madame Blaise's table.

"You would not recognize him, Gliesli; and when I complain he just says, 'Our habits are changing because we are getting old.' And now, on account of his British doggedness and pigheadedness, he persists in it. He reads all through the meal. I started to do a thing I have never done, I brought a book to the table. But he did not mind: he read all through that meal. We do not exchange a single word; and after lunch he goes up, and fifteen minutes later he is asleep on the lounge with the sun pouring on his face; and there he rests until it is time for our tea. Ah, if you had known him only three years ago, in Malaya, you would not recognize him now."

In the afternoon before he went to sleep, he said irritably to Lilia:

"Do go in and see that woman next to me; she is knocking on the wall again. Does she suppose I am going to visit her?"

"I told her to knock if she wanted anything, and you would call me."

"And yet you do nothing but fuss about people knowing our relationship!"

"But this is a case of sickness."

Robert laughed impertinently, lay down on the lounge and put a handkerchief over his face.

"Robert, I myself don't feel well. I think I must see a doctor."

"Oh, I think you will pull through."

"Robert, your unkindness is killing me. I can feel my love slowly dying."

"Lilia, go and exorcise that blessed poltergeist. I shall have her moved."

Lilia went quickly away, heart struck by his unflinching cruelty. Miss Chillard required some trifling service. Afterwards Mrs. Trollope went down to the office, and though I was at work she interrupted me to tell me about her health and ask if I knew a reliable doctor. "Madame Blaise knows one, but I am becoming a little wary about her advice. I wish Mr. Wilkins would see a doctor; I am sure he is getting liverish."

I gave her the addresses of two doctors and told her to use the telephone. Mrs. Trollope began to weep; she put her arms around my neck and said:

"Oh, dear Madame, I hope you will never be as unhappy as I am. You will never know, thank God, my agony and shame."

"Everyone admires and respects you both, I assure you."

"Ah, but I don't feel it. What have I done to live like this? Mr. Wilkins was so delightful to me before. Now I think he is just a photograph in a window: he seems to stand up, but he is held up by a bit of cardboard. He is nice to look at and seems kind and cheerful, but if that were so, how could all this be? What did you think of me, when I came and asked you for two rooms communicating, and us with different names; and said we were cousins, though we at once began to live a married life? He always makes me do it. He will not go himself first. And I am obliged to call him my cousin. Thank God there are more kind people in the world than you would imagine. Can you imagine, Selda, what my feelings were that day?"

"Really, you exaggerate. You are unwell and so you feel low in spirits. Everyone likes you."

"I don't think life is worthy of us. If I did not have my religion, I could not drag myself along another mile of my road. For example, that money in the safe: he will not give it to me. He says I am just a child, a babe in the woods."

"You must insist upon getting your own money, Madame."

"In Malaya you see, he told me, 'Do not worry, Lilia, I have provided for you. My will is always kept up to date and you will benefit by it. You will never have to worry.' I always said, 'Oh, my dear one, my beloved one, do not mention these things to me. I cannot discuss such terrible things with you, your will and what it all means.' But he always came back to it: 'Do not worry, Lilia, you will get a large share of my money, because of what you have been to me; and you will never have a thing to think about.' I was contented just the same and did not say anything. But, Madame, when my husband, Mr. Trollope, gave my money back into my hands at the time of the divorce, and provided for his three children, too, Robert changed. He suggested we should come abroad. I did not know why, but I thought, knowing his mother's objections, that we would get married quietly and no one would suffer for it. But I did not mention it to him—it was a delicate subject. Well, when he returned to Yorkshire at last, to see the family he had not seen for over twenty years, he said not a word about me, and they were pleased. They thought that at last he had got rid of me and was coming home to them and to spend his money on them. So these three or four poor old women told everyone that Robert had now retired and was coming home from the East and was going to help with the garden and to can raspberries and to help them with the sick bedridden old mother. I must not say anything against them. I loved Robert and it is such a pain to me—they had always despised that East he worked in and in one room he found all the cases and packages he had ever sent them. I think they were afraid to undo them for fear of catching an eastern disease. But who knows? I myself, Madame, sent them silks and carved boxes. Then, when they found out, they refused to believe that I was divorced, because I am a Catholic; and when Robert went to the pantry door to get me a jar of chutney, homemade English chutney they had made, Chrissie, the eldest sister, locked the pantry door in his face and said: 'It will rot there rather. Not one thing of ours will go to that woman. You may have it but you may not share it with her.'

"Robert was very angry—you do not know him. This is one of the reasons I cannot talk to him, he has an ugly temper—he was so angry that he went to his satchel and took out a long envelope. Out of the envelope he took his latest will which he showed to them. He made them put on their glasses to look at it and said: 'This is my last will and testament. In it I named you four beneficiaries and you were generously provided for. Now, this is what I do.' And before their eyes he tore the thick paper into little pieces, collected the pieces and burnt them in the fireplace."

"Well, that's all right," I said to Mrs. Trollope.

"But in that will, Madame, I was named for my share and you see they will now inherit everything as next of kin and there will be endless trouble if Robert should die intestate. What am I saying? Think what has happened to me to bring me to say such a thing! He has never made a will since. You don't understand why I worry. He has a lot of my property in his hands; he controls it and can make it his if he wants to. For since the time we left Malaya he has made every effort to get my property slowly into his hands. He has so changed."

Mrs. Trollope wrung her hands.

"All that I held onto myself is some ten thousand pounds which I am gradually bringing to Switzerland. But now I have refused to bring out anymore. Supposing I am left alone? And he can't forgive me. I gave him control of everything in the beginning, for I thought of him as my husband. I don't want to wander all over the world and calculate those 'switches' as Robert calls them. I would rather lose half my money. He does not trust me now. I have made such arrangements with him that I cannot get my money back without a lawsuit. And that I could never bring myself to do."

"Go to a lawyer anyway, it won't come to a lawsuit," I said, looking at her face, and troubled.

Suddenly, she exclaimed: "Why, it's getting dark! Oh, what did the poor sparrows think of me? Robert must be waiting for his drink. He never drinks without me."

She ran upstairs.

Upstairs she said: "Oh, Robert, let us think of somewhere better to go. Let us find a livelier place."

"Yes. You know, out there, I fancied I could never drink anything but whisky, and then you know, the few small gins half an hour before dinner. And I've got quite used to them; but I fancy I could change."

"Oh, Robert, I have never got used to this lonely life. Out there, people were dropping in all day. I was happy all day, laughing. You remember? Here it is silence from morning to night. I never had to think of getting friends; and I had my dear children with me. Now, I talk to anyone."

"Well, perhaps next year we will go to Tangiers or Marrakesh. I don't want you to feel miserable."

"That is a very kind word, Robert."

"If you buy me the car," said Robert.

But the next morning Mrs. Trollope came back looking very tired. She had been to church, where she had spent a very long time praying to Saint Anselm, her own particular saint. Her name as a girl had been Anselm. Somehow she had got no hope from him. She had begged him to show her what to do about Robert and her future life; she had begged him too to help her in finding the lost hundred francs; but no help had come to her.

She had gone to the hairdresser's where she met Madame Blaise, and afterwards they had taken too long a walk. Madame Blaise had gone into one of the big jewelers in town, and though she was always short of cash she had had a hundred-franc note changed, when she bought some of the snake rings they were all mad about then.

She lay down after lunch, for that evening they had the dinner for the Blaises, to which they had now also invited the Pallintosts and their acquaintance Princess Bili di Rovino, who had just come back to the hotel. The Princess was an American, rich, old and the widow of an Italian prince. Lilia said to Robert:

"I am going later to spend the afternoon with the Princess. We are having tea at the Lausanne Palace. Shall you come?"

"Oh, I don't know, Lilia. I went to the bank this morning and I don't know what is the matter with that chap; his rates are wrong. So I must go this afternoon and see the manager."

"The Princess thought you were going to take Angel for a walk," said Lilia, referring to the Princess's pet Sealyham. "Couldn't you take him with you to the bank? I should like to have a quiet chat with Bili."

"Oh, I hate to be bothered with any more nonsense about Angel. Yesterday I had to buy him a worm-powder and a leash. Do you think I enjoyed that?"

"Yes, but the Princess has been so good to us."

"No, I shall not take him to the bank."

"But you know the Princess must leave him in her room. He howls; well, she says he is singing; and he spoils the bedcovers and they are going to charge her double. Do please, Robert, take him; you promised."

"Oh, very well; but it's a nuisance; and I shall lose my nap."

When Mr. Wilkins had gone off to get the dog, Mrs. Trollope lay down and called Luisa, who was counting the hotel laundry.

"I am too nervous, Luisa, to sleep. So tell me when you are going to take your holiday. I don't know what I'm going to do without you with my poor head. But then you need it. Look at your legs."

"I am not going to take my holiday," said Luisa shortly.

"Why not?"

"I don't wish to."

"You can't work the whole year day and night and take no holiday."

"I don't wish to. It doesn't please me."

"You don't want to see your mother, father, fiancé, your little sister?"

Mrs. Trollope heard Clara out on the landing and called her:
"Clara, come here, venez ici."

She expostulated, explained that Luisa would not go and see her parents. She kissed Luisa on the cheek and hand, begged her to go, said she did not know what a mother felt, told Clara she must force Luisa to go. The wiry weathered blonde grinned, stood with her arms akimbo, said in her slapdash manner:

"You are quite right, Luisa, not to take your holiday. I had two weeks' holiday in the beginning of the year and I assure you I only just got my bones undone when I had to put them together again; and when I came back it took me a week to recover. Now, Thursday was my day off and I spent the whole day in bed. That made me unfit for work. On Friday I felt worse and I took some vermouth with Charlie, so that things would not look so black, and on Saturday I felt worse than Friday. The same thing when you sleep. Lots of nights you don't sleep. Then you can easily get up at six, but you don't feel well; and you walk about with your eyes half shut. People are not to be blamed for thinking you went

81

on the binge the night before. Other nights you sleep and you try to wake up at six; but it is perfect misery; you wish you were dead. One morning I overslept, Madame bawled me out; the next night I stayed up all night; at least I was good and drunk at six o'clock; and things didn't seem bad; but later on, oh, my. So what is the use of sleeping, what is the use of a day off, what is the use of holidays? Work until you drop, until the doctor has to come, I say; and then perhaps you can get a whole month's holiday in bed, which is the only place to spend it. Once I broke my legs on the stairs and got three months' holiday. Now Charlie nearly broke his back, has had a floating kidney, and his heart is thumping, and I think it was carrying the new elevator up from the lower street level, where they left it. Mr. Bonnard said: 'Bring up the lift, Charlie.' I saw him and I said: 'You're crazy, Charlie, let it rot downstairs; let them get some men. You're a porter but not an elephant. Why don't they ask you to shift the whole hotel to another site?' He said: 'I used to be able to lift more than this, I was so strong, but now I'm sixty-nine.' I said: 'You're mad, Charlie; no one will wear his eyes out weeping for you when you're dead; even I won't. I'll say, That crazy Charlie.' He said: 'Oh, they expect me to do it.' Then he was in bed ten days. I swear that finished him. He's a wreck now. They'll throw him out of here. But he said: 'You see, I got ten days in bed.' I said: 'They'll throw you out for loafing on them.' He said: 'So I'll get a good rest before I take to the road.' Eh! What do you think of that, Madame?"

Luisa said: "You see, Madame, I like a holiday at home; but my sister is married and can only see her husband two weeks a year; so this year she can have my holiday too, four weeks."

The two servants went out and began again on the laundry lists.

Mrs. Trollope turned restlessly till it was time to get up. She was nervous and undecided what to tell Princess Bili. She had made Bili a promise before Bili's last trip to Rome; and she had not been able to carry it out. Presently she went out up the hill and met the Princess in the tearoom, where they had a long talk; and then they both came back to the little hotel, to get the dog. Bili took the dog from Mr. Wilkins and went to her room till it was time for drinks. Mrs. Trollope went to her room.

"I'm afraid Bili insists upon bringing Angel to the dinner. She thinks someone may see Angel and want him."

"Oh, blast Angel. Do you know what happened? You know that leash I bought him yesterday for two francs fifty. I was sitting on the bench on the esplanade; and he chewed it off and ate it right up to my wrist. I had to buy him another which cost me six francs fifty."

"He is such a naughty boy. I knew that thin leash would not hold him."

Lilia went into her room and shut the door. It was not long before she heard Madame Blaise's signal.

"Liliali, wherever have you been? Come and fix my hair for me, something special for dinner. If we are to have the Princess with us and the English people. Dr. Blaise and I fancied we were going to dine with you alone."

"Oh, Robert thought we would have an all-in party; it will be gayer."

At five-thirty they passed through the two doors into Mr. Wilkins's room as usual for their drinks. About six-thirty there was a knock at the door and in came the Princess in dinner dress, leading Angel by the new leash bought by Mr. Wilkins that afternoon.

"Bili, I do wish you would leave that dog at home," said Mr. Wilkins.

The Princess exclaimed at once:

"Now, Robert, do not make a fuss about poor Angel. I cannot leave him at the hotel. He has been running up and downstairs all day, no one could catch him, he ran in and out of the dining room and kitchen. He is so very naughty. The maids say they won't go into our room to make up our beds, for he runs out. Then when I am away they say he practices singing to try to call me back. Sometimes he howls sadly, they say, and the guests complain. There are old people in these hotels who are very touchy. Herr Altstadt complained today. He knows us and he will be good with us. Everyone loves you, Angel."

The old doctor smiled maliciously, while Mr. Wilkins looked down his nose.

Madame Blaise said: "Lilia, why didn't you tell me you were going to dress? I shall go and put on my new hat. You know you prevented me from wearing it and now I shall ruin my lovely hairdo."

Lilia, after looking for a moment, said:

"Bili, we weren't dressing, dear."

Bili said: "Oh, I got dressed now; I can't undress. I shall stay as I am; no one will mind. Why don't you put on a dinner dress, Lilia?"

"Please go back and change, Princess," said Mr. Wilkins drily.

"I really feel myself this way; do let's have a pleasant evening," said the Princess.

They argued with her and it ended with Madame Blaise going out to put on her new hat, and Mrs. Trollope changing her dress. The Princess remained. The setting sun shone from their right into the room, and the Princess standing at the window could see an enormous Roman pillar of fire, immensely high, apparently reaching beyond the lake into the deep mist which hung above it and hid the mountains of Haute-Savoie. The sun was pale blood-red and so was the pillar of fire. Flights of sparrows flying home dispersed as raindrops. In a few minutes the first bat would appear. Blackbirds were tinkling and fighting round the lawns and trees. The setting sun made a pillar of fire of the Princess too, a tall figure surrounded with small running fires.

Her bright yellow hair was dressed with flowers and gauze. She wore a pink tulle and silk dinner gown, very décolleté, an amethyst necklace, a spray of silk wisteria diagonally across the left breast to the stomach. This spray she had added herself, to match the necklace. She had amethyst suede gloves wrinkled to the elbow, numerous expensive bracelets and pretty little burgundy shoes. For a moment she was a delightful vision, for the sun glared on the glass, a vision of youth; thus for a moment she was what she wished to be, young, beautiful and wonderfully dressed. A second look showed her cavernous blue eyes, the heavy flesh-colored makeup, the thin cords and the other marks of her years. Even as they saw her, she was a remarkable creation; a painter would have painted her. There was not only a reminiscence of vivid youth in her dress, but something burning still; a burning glass that looked through the rags and tatters of her flesh. They knew very little about her. Mrs. Trollope and Mr. Wilkins had met her some years ago on the Côte d'Azur, been taken up by her. She fascinated Lilia with her chatter of race courses, stock exchange boardrooms, promoters, automobile owners, millionaire owners of horseflesh, all fashionable society; and she knew not only the elegants, the cream, but the go-betweens, those one has to know to get money exchanged at the best rate, little private businesses done. She interested Mr. Wilkins too with this.

The Blaises had only just met her.

Mr. Wilkins said:

"I say, Bili, you will put us all to shame. Do go and put on something suitable. I assure you it is just an ordinary restaurant in Lausanne. You will look like the Queen of England at a ragpickers' tea. You have time; please do as I say."

"No, I shall not disappoint myself just to please you, Robert. I know what is behind it. You are a Protestant and pinched, you want life to be a suit of dull gray. I know what is done and worn. I have moved in the most fashionable circles in Cannes, Nice, Biarritz and in Rome; and I do not see why I should not wear a dinner dress when I get a chance."

"But, my dear Bili, this is a ball dress."

"Oh, what nonsense, Robert. You were never at a ball in your life."

Mrs. Trollope laughed and said:

"That is quite true. Robert hates balls and only likes to dance in bars and cabarets. But you must remember, Bili, that now in Paris you can practically go to a ball in a tailormade."

"Not in the Paris I know," said the Princess, lifting her head so that the dewdropped tulle and the little butterflies twinkled.

They were having a drink, when in came Madame Blaise with a beautiful evening hat, on a toque of feathers and gauze with two drooping plumes and a diamond in her hair. It was a French hat and the diamond looked well in Madame Blaise's hair; but Dr. Blaise took exception to the getup, said the hat did not suit her dress, nor the occasion, and certainly not the Princess's costume.

The Princess said: "We women shall do just as we please and I shall make Angel sing, too. You two drab men have nothing to think about but making money and you are not the arbiters of taste. I assure you we are not going to have our evening spoiled for you. Lilia dear, let us go and make you up. You look so tired, and being constantly in the sun and wind has done nothing for your skin."

"Now you know quite well, Bili, there's scarcely a breath of wind here for days," said Mr. Wilkins.

Nevertheless, the Princess installed Lilia before a looking glass in the next room, shut the door and the hum of their voices could be heard for some time. The men paid no attention and they and Mrs. Blaise were talking about where they should move their main funds, to the Argentine, Colombia, the United States, South Africa? No one thought it was going to be safe in the end to leave them in Switzerland. How long would the world allow Switzerland to remain neutral? Switzerland was gorged with gold: wasn't that too great a temptation?

Said Mr. Wilkins: "I have transferred my pounds into dollars and Swiss francs and if I could induce some fellow to say his country was going to withdraw all his funds from the U.S.A., or to make an investigation into financial skullduggery in this country, or if I could get some dictator or president to declare that Switzerland is going to be first victim in the next war—so that the Swiss franc would drop and we could get it cheap—then we would be rich, transfer back into dollars, go abroad—for I do not think Switzerland is safe at all. About this gold hoard in the mountains, there are only four or five persons know its whereabouts—one of them must be a friend of the Russians, there's always one—if the Russians want the money they'll take it; and if they don't want it they'll blow it sky high to ruin us all. Eh? And the Swiss franc falls to less than the weight of paper overnight."

Meanwhile the Princess said: "I had to get you alone, Lilia; did you put the question to him?"

"I could not, Bili. It is so hard for me. I can't ask him to marry me. It's so bold. I couldn't do it."

They conversed for some time about this.

Presently, Lilia came in made up by the Princess. Her dark skin was creamed a thick pale olive matt and thickly powdered with a pale rachel powder, her eyebrows were unnaturally arched, a small birthmark obliterated, the hairline had been curved into a widow's peak, she wore mascara. Her fingernails, generally a dark alabaster or pale pink, were now rose red.

"Good God, Lilia, is that you?" said Mr. Wilkins.

"I told you, Bili," said Lilia in an agony.

"Lilia looks lovely; but naturally you don't want her to be truly attractive to other men," said the Princess.

"Oh, fiddlesticks," said Mr. Wilkins.

In the end poor Lilia, in tears, with her mascara already running, went back wiped it all off and went off with them with nothing but a trace of dark powder and lipstick and on her head a black scarf run with gold thread. Her face was weary from the trials of the day and evening.

When they got downstairs, the Pallintosts, an English couple in their mid-thirties, Aline and Tony, were waiting in the little parlor, which became a second dining room in the busy season.

The drive uptown, though short, was pleasant. The doctor was a smooth fast driver. Mr. Wilkins sat in front with him. They did not discuss business with the three women there. Mr. Wilkins charmingly discussed what was proper at that time of the day and in those circumstances, in the East—various old eastern acquaintances, football and polo games he had played and witnessed in the last thirty-five years. He not only pretended to be but he was an unassuming man; and to be an unassuming man of his worth was his highest ambition. His other ambition, the making of a modest but solid, respectable fortune, he had almost achieved.

They drew up in front of the Grand Café, which is on the plateau at the other end of the big square; and they went into the fashionable bar, which, as it runs around a corner, is most inconvenient, but smart enough; and which, at this hour, was nearly filled with well-dressed Swiss. Madame Blaise no longer wore her pretty hat, she had had to change it; and she looked dowdy, for she was wearing on top of her jacket and short coat a third covering, a worn mink coat. The Princess also wore a mink coat and for the moment did not look out of place, though underneath dressed as for the opera; and Mrs. Trollope, in her modest clothes, looked like a good serious little bourgeoise trotting along behind two pretentious friends.

They sat down in a corner near the café door and ordered drinks. At this moment they were joined by the Pallintosts, who had come in their car behind. Dr. Blaise then told the waiter that they had a table reserved for seven—a little odd that he mentioned it first, for it was Mr. Wilkins's table; but as Mr. Wilkins made a show of not speaking French (he spoke it rather well but slowly and precisely), the guests thought it perhaps a clumsy courtesy of Dr. Blaise. Another waiter came up with a tablet and menu and asked them what they would take for hors d'oeuvre. Oh, no hors d'oeuvre, said the Pallintosts, who had also talked over between themselves the propriety of their being asked at all; and going ahead, pressed by the doctor, they ordered two cheap dishes of different sorts, just as they had decided beforehand; Aline took one a little dearer, Tony one a little cheaper, just above the cheapest of all.

"Have you smoked salmon, some real caviar Malossol, some Douarnenez sardines? I had them last time I was here," said the doctor.

The waiter went off to bring the maître d'hôtel. The doctor

passed the menu to the Pallintosts. They refused. "Nothing, really nothing, but the main dish."

Out of politeness, then, Mr. Wilkins said he would take a sardine too. He insisted on more drinks. The maître d'hôtel arrived to show a fine piece of smoked Rhine salmon; and as it pleased the doctor he also suggested pâté de foie gras from Périgord. The doctor assented:

"Certainly, I always have it when I come here."

Dr. Blaise went on at once to order fish, meat, salad for himself and his wife; and asked for the wine waiter. The table, noses in drinks, was a little confused and intimidated. The Pallintosts stuck to their plan, the wife ordering sweetbreads, and the husband a veal cutlet. Mr. Wilkins, seeing what was happening, then insisted upon Pallintost ordering an entrecôte which was about the middle of the bill in price, and the rest took roast chicken, except for the Blaises, who had ordered partridge and tournedos Rossini.

The little meal had taken on another air. When the wine waiter came, the doctor made a hasty canvass. The Pallintosts refused wine, Mrs. Trollope said she hated it, Mr. Wilkins said he would have some, but rather pointedly consulted Mrs. Pallintost's taste; and she, pressed, said she preferred red, though she knew white was correct for sweetbreads. After Mr. Wilkins had ordered a bottle of local rosé wine, Dr. Blaise impatiently handed the card to the wine waiter and ordered two bottles of an excellent Alsatian wine called Dambacher for the others, and a bottle, for himself, of the Swiss white wine known as Johannisberger, vintage 1945. Nevertheless, there was no question of Dr. and Madame Blaise fancying that they were part hosts; for they knew something that the Pallintosts did not, that this was the anniversary of the day, twenty-seven years before, when Mrs. Trollope, a beautiful innocent young wife with Egyptian eyes and a fine skin, an elegant little creature, had met Mr. Wilkins, a goodlooking strong little Englishman, with yellow hair, a high color and red lips. He was a business acquaintance of her husband. They had danced together that evening and fallen in love, as it seemed to them later, at once. Mr. Trollope, a tall, thin faced but agreeable Englishman, already rich, was at the time courting two or three other women and had a passion for an Indian dancer. Several years later, Mrs. Trollope left her husband, the scandal being too public; and from that time on, she and Robert Wilkins had been close friends. This early part of their history was unknown to most people; and Mr. Wilkins had always been called "our father's friend" by the children of Mrs. Trollope. About five years before this evening, Mr. Trollope, after a long series of romances, found he wished to marry a local woman with money and allowed Mrs. Trollope to divorce him; couching his offer in these words:

"You may divorce me for infidelity, Lilia; for I have no complaint against you."

Their three children, now adult, and two married, were in the British Isles. Mrs. Trollope then went to Europe with Mr. Wilkins, expecting to marry him at once. But all love affairs hold surprises, including those of such long standing that they resemble marriages. Mr. Wilkins remained her lover, lived beside her, but made her engage their lodgings wherever they lived and pay their rent. She had never before engaged rooms or paid rent. She said, deeply shocked:

"But people will think you are my gigolo."

"That is most flattering for a man of my age."

All the details of this affair, unknown to her children, Mrs. Trollope, in her agony of mind, had confided not only to the Princess in Nice, but now to Madame Blaise.

The company, because of the embarrassment and the unusual amount of alcohol, became slightly fogged. Mrs. Trollope and Mr. Wilkins presently led the way into and through the large café, asking for their table at the other end of the restaurant. It was a very large place, modern, cheerful, with a high gilded and carved roof; and divided into several sorts of cafés and eating places. At the far end was a more expensive section, arranged in a series of alcoves, with a heavy carved canopy in which hung lamps. In the alcoves were mirrors, candle brackets, colored steel engravings.

Dr. Blaise, at one end, sat next to the Princess, then Madame Blaise, then Tony Pallintost, his wife, Mrs. Trollope and, last, Mr. Wilkins.

The Princess sat under a hunting print with her dog beside her.

They began to eat their hors d'oeuvre. Dr. Blaise poured out the Johannisberger for himself and his wife, the Dambacher for the others and told the wine waiter to fetch another bottle of Johannisberger, a dear wine. Madame Blaise remarked with satisfaction:

"It's my husband's favorite wine; he always drinks it when he has a chance. He has a caseful at home, which he locks away; but

I am not so fond of it." At this she raised her full glass and took a mouthful, swilled it round her mouth, gulped it down and set her glass down empty. The waiter filled it again.

Dr. Blaise told him to fill the other glasses; they protested but thanked Mr. Wilkins, while the doctor smiled, and they drank. Mr. Wilkins insisted upon his soup, and after seven or eight remarks, the doctor persuaded the Pallintosts and the Princess, who were tired of looking at their empty plates, to have some pâté de foie, exceptionally fine. Eventually he induced Mrs. Pallintost and the Princess to have some caviar also; though the others refused. Madame Blaise seconded her husband in what was now quite clearly an attempt to pile on the expense and had her plate heaped with various delicacies. She ate soup, on second thoughts ordered some fera, a fine salmon-colored lake fish, and others joined her. In the meantime a second bottle of Johannisberger had been ordered by the doctor; and when Mr. Wilkins said, "Oh, there is some other white wine there not opened yet," the doctor laughed in a noisy hostile way: "Johannisberger is my favorite wine and I am going to have a good time; as well be hung for a sheep as a lamb."

"We are not going to be hung, I hope," said Mrs. Trollope.

The Princess said: "We will be, if the Russians get us. If they saw us having a dinner like this, we should at once be stood up against a wall and shot, not even a drumhead court-martial."

Mr. Wilkins laughed. "But Bili, civilians do not get a drumhead court-martial."

"Well, a committee of public safety."

"No, it is called the Politburo," said Mr. Pallintost.

They discussed, over the fish, the kind of committee, if any, to be instituted by the Russians when they came to Switzerland to take their money and their lives, and Mrs. Trollope said sadly:

"Oh, I wonder where we will all be next year. We don't have a home anymore, do we? In the old days you were at least safe in your own country. Now the Russians and their friends are everywhere. Would you believe it, Mrs. Pallintost, there are communists in the British Civil Service. They have found them and are going to root them out. Oh, I could never have believed such a thing of Englishmen. I saw it in the papers or I should never have believed the story. What can be the matter? I am distracted with worry."

The Princess said: "I know where I shall be. I shall be in the Argentine. It is nice there. They have plenty of food and it is safe for us."

Madame Blaise said: "And they have plenty of gigolos."

She had taken several glasses of wine. She opened her handbag and brought out a sheaf of photographs of all sizes. Looking at her husband with a roll of her handsome eyes, she laughed:

"I must have gigolos, for these are the kind of gigolos my husband brings me home. My husband talks to me about nothing but diseases. He talks of different things to his men friends; but to me, only infection, vitiated blood, pus, syphilis, gonorrhoea, diabetes, psoriasis, scrofula, cancer. Look at the pretty pictures he is always giving me;" and laughing heartily, her big bosom wallowing, she handed Mr. Pallintost a photograph of a naked boy of about sixteen, with face and entire body skin covered with a crepy red tissue. She said: "Show it to Mrs. Pallintost. How would you like to have to look at that every evening?"

Mrs. Pallintost diffidently took it and passed it onto the Princess.

"What is it, a fishboy?" said the Princess.

"Oh, I think it's the result of diabetes and may be cured with insulin," said the doctor carelessly.

Madame Blaise was now passing round the table pictures of children with blue patches, men with psoriasis, and a late stage of cancer in a woman. Mr. Pallintost began rejecting them, but the Princess seized them one after the other, glanced and passed them on. The doctor in the end took them himself, scrutinized them and handed them back, very nicely at times and at other times with a grimace of horror; and once he hissed, once moaned. But it was hard to tell what he felt. When this batch of photographs had gone the rounds, three family photographs followed them, one of Dr. Blaise and his son Hubert, a man of about twenty-four, fat, fair and smiling. (Madame Blaise said: "Do you see the likeness. Oh, he couldn't accuse me then of gigolos!") One was of Hubert stepping into the first car she had bought him and one of Hubert holding the head of a stallion his mother had recently bought him. These and others went round and passed back into the gaping crocodile skin of the huge bag, which had crocodile claws on both sides.

By this time the main dishes had begun to come in, and before each guest stood the silver chafing dishes, heated by squat candles, which the Swiss use. The waiter and captain were about them, helping, offering, suggesting; the wines were poured, the rosé, the Dambacher and some more Johannisberger was brought for the doctor and his wife. Again Dr. Blaise was making suggestions:

"Why not a few french fried with that? Why not ask for some oyster-plant if you like it so much?"

In the course of conversation he had drawn out the special tastes of the guests. Mr. Wilkins then politely repeated the suggestions and the waiters were kept busy. So they had various salads; many cheeses were brought. Afterwards the doctor and his wife took crêpes suzette, though no one else was hungry; and after this the coffee, and the doctor had already ordered a fourth bottle of Johannisberger; though Mr. Wilkins said, rather less mildly than before:

"I thought we had enough wine; but I am not a wine drinker and neither is my cousin."

The doctor bluffly called the wine waiter and ordered two more bottles, and not one.

The doctor was a strong short man, with dark hair partly gray, dyed perhaps; he was slightly bowed by age or by bending over patients' beds, or by his own paunch, about sixty, brisk, clean, merry, malicious, with a firm chin. Madame Blaise now brought out of her crocodile bag her last letter from her son Hubert, now in the U.S.A. on a ranch, where she had bought him a small private plane. She and he kept telegraphing each other. He was looking after her affairs and wanted her advice on his joining a publicity firm. The doctor during this conversation became seedy and tired. He said suddenly to Mr. Pallintost:

"All marriage is hell, don't you think? Aren't you the slave of a woman? Don't you agree, Mrs. Pallintost, that marriage is a curse? But you like to have a man as your slave, I suppose."

"If there is any slave, I suppose we are both slaves, we are both the same," said she.

Madame Blaise liked this conversation. She said:

"My son has only gone away from me because he was engaged to a girl and I could never allow that. I would rather he took his chance. Horses, cars and flying are dangerous and he may get killed; but it is not like losing my son to another woman. I prefer him to love men and on ranches I heard there are plenty in fancy boots. So I made him go; and once he is corrupted he will never turn back; he may marry but he will hate and torture the bitch. My daughter's a clown. She married a fat young professor, a real capon; he couldn't have a child, and they adopted one. I never wanted a daughter; they are all frumps; and she will get nothing from me. Now, the stupid sow has taken a

92

lover. In this family they all flounder about; the only action in the family comes from me."

"You'd like to see them both die," snarled the doctor.

"I'd like to see him die, rather than see him tied to another woman. He is the only person I ever loved. Isn't it my right, Lilia darling? Isn't it my right, Mrs. Pallintost? My husband never loved me. He married me for my money. He was a ragged student. When he married me he had never had a woman and he married me to see what a woman was like. I mean, a woman who had a very large dowry."

"To get you when you were only thirty-three and find you a virgin was very lucky," said the doctor, smiling horribly.

"And you never had a woman and really it was the same always as if you had never had one," said Madame Blaise.

"So you say, but how can you know?" said the doctor. With a hearty misplaced laugh, he snapped his fingers for the wine waiter. He ordered some brandy for himself and his wife and asked the others; but no one responded, until pressed by Mr. Wilkins, when a glass each was brought for Mrs. Trollope and the Princess. The doctor turned to Pallintost and said frankly and with some honesty:

"I came from a hungry farm, I went bootless to school. I had to work my way through medical school. I had the good luck to marry an heiress. The rest is my own."

The Princess had had Angel, her sealyham, on the geranium-colored cushion beside her during dinner, feeding him titbits. The manager had brought him a plate of meat and some water, so that Angel had behaved very well up to now. But now the Princess said:

"But we have not made Angel sing. You know, Mrs. Pallintost, I am trying to sell Angel, for I must go away to South America. I do not know what restrictions there are. But I want him in good hands. I want someone who will see him as he is. I have advertised him and had plenty of offers for him, but unfortunately I have left his pedigree at home in Italy, I do not know where; and my Italian maids are darlings, they adore me, simply worship the ground I walk on, for it means nothing to us, but a great deal to them, poor dears, it really lightens their work, that they are working for a Princess; and I know they pray for me in church. Still, they can hardly read or write and I am sure they would not understand a document like Angel's pedigree. So it is no use writing to them."

"But write to the General's wife," said Mrs. Trollope.

"You and Robert really should go and stay in my apartment. It is so comfortable, warm, excluding the heating, it would only cost you 10,000 lire a month. You would save money and have a darling personal maid, Teresa, an unmarried mother with a boy at high school who will simply do anything, sewing and cutting out and all you must pay her is 11,000 lire a month; and a little something extra for dresses if you wish it; and you don't pay the whole expenses but share with the General and his wife. And before they were married the General got on ideally with Teresa and Maria, that's Teresa's sister who comes in; you pay her about 10,000 lire, it depends; and it cost the General only 20,000 lire a month, all in. Of course, the poor man—"

"Yes, Bili—" Mrs. Trollope tried to interrupt.

But the Princess went on with the General's family history for a long time and accounted for all the General's family expenses, which they could share.

"How old was the General's mother, the Countess?" asked Mrs. Trollope.

"Ninety-six, but she had all her faculties and though she was so small, like a little child, I assure you he could have carried her in his pocket, I assure you she was very spry and did all the accounts and was carried off only by a cold: there was nothing the matter with her. The General did not know what to do. He had lived for her. He sent for my friend who was in Bogota because she was afraid of the Russians, she felt she could not go back to Columbus, Ohio; but when he told her about the big empty apartment she came and married him."

"Oh, Bili, Robert and I are thinking of going to South America, but the idea makes me very unhappy," said Mrs. Trollope.

"That's why I thought my apartment in Milan would be ideal for you. They are all so simple; they adore us."

Said Lilia: "Well, it is a question of my pounds. I do not want to bring them all abroad. Robert thinks I am stupid; but I say to him, I don't care if I lose some money. I cannot live for the exchanges, I want to live in peace. I want some money in my homeland, and if the pound is getting smaller and smaller as they say I still want some of it somewhere in the British Empire. Do you know, Robert has a chart; he will show it to you only too willingly. He works on it every day; all his business ability has come down to that; and it shows that all the exchanges are against the pound, as he expresses it. All over the world at a given moment, we, that is the pound, may be weak. It amuses him; and this chart is to be the chart of my life."

Robert laughed modestly:

"Well, it's like crosswords, you see. I like it. It reminds me of business; and besides, I have not yet entirely concluded my business in Malaya. And it makes me sleep well. If Lilia would take an interest, she is really very good at it, she would sleep better."

Mrs. Trollope continued: "If I want half a dozen of those pretty Swiss handkerchiefs for Jessamine my married daughter, I do not hear a word from him for a whole hour and then he brings me a calculation of what it would cost me in France, England, South Africa, the Argentine and the U.S.A. and how I must transfer the pounds to pay for it. I do not want to understand. Surely it is very easy, if you have money? Surely I can enjoy my own money without this? But you see, for Robert, it is his only genuine pleasure; it is his hobby."

Robert was flattered. "Oh, you see, Mrs. Pallintost, we are getting older; and I am not so energetic as I was. It keeps my memory and faculties working. Don't you find your memory failing, for example, Mrs. Pallintost?"

Mrs. Pallintost, who was thirty-five, said:

"No, my memory is quite all right."

"How is your memory? Do you remember why you left Basel?" said the doctor, laughing, to his wife.

"Well, mine isn't what it was," said Mr. Wilkins complacently.

Mr. Pallintost introduced the subject of the car he wanted Mr. Wilkins to buy. Mr. Wilkins went into a long description of the car, the body, the engine, the peculiar advantages of the selling prices in Switzerland and elsewhere, the course of the exchanges over the past few months, what he could get it for now if the manufacturers had stuck to their bargain, for even if they did not, he had allowed a small margin for the fall of the lira. He also said he had in mind a car he had just seen in the Geneva show, a Fiat whippet or midget very suitable for them, with seats for two in front and very roomy in the back for luggage.

"I should never have to offer anyone a lift; I should never have more than one passenger, my cousin Lilia. And very roomy in the back for luggage."

He and Mrs. Trollope argued about how much luggage they could stow in the back—"certainly not my steamer trunk"—and how far they could go with it.

Everyone became interested, discussed how far the whippet

would go, what hills it could climb and whether it was suitable for Switzerland in winter. Mr. Wilkins said: "But that is just where I intend to use it. I am a good driver and if I tip Lilia over the edge of some Alp that will be just an accident." He laughed gaily, rubbing his hands, and continued:

"But I hardly think it will come to that. I should hardly like to kill Lilia in a car where she has put me at the wheel of her own free will. Lilia has put me at the wheel of her fortune and I think I shall manage both with reasonable skill."

Mrs. Trollope said restlessly: "I would rather trust myself than anyone. Robert no doubt means well, but he cannot keep his hands off money. He is always wanting to try those charts of his on money. And it is my money he experiments with. I may be old-fashioned; I am, I know. But I think money is stable. It is what you have. It is what you live by. I don't like it parcelled out and fooled with. Now I had money coming to me in France last year and I wrote a letter to the people saying I would accept it in francs. The people wrote back saying they would pay me in francs at once. And Robert made me write another clever letter saying they must get permission from the exchange, permission to pay me in England where the money was due; and then Robert intended to change it into Swiss francs at the permitted rate and I could get my French dress in French francs exchanged for Swiss francs at the black-market rate, and do you know what happened? They have not made arrangements to pay me from that day to this."

"Oh, I knew that story was coming. Lilia cannot get it into her head—" and he began explaining patiently as if Lilia had not understood; but she put her hands to her head and said:

"I should rather lose half the money than go through all that."

Mr. Wilkins said gently: "But, Lilia, that is it; I do not want you to lose half your money; and I am going to see that you increase it. Neither of us is young anymore and we must think of our old age."

The Princess cried: "I think that kind of talk is mad, Robert. As soon as I sell Angel, I am going off to the Argentine and I am going to get married. First, of course, I have an appointment in Paris next month, where I am going to have a certain operation, and when I have spent some weeks in a nursing home I shall be young again and I am going to South America where they have dictators and an organized society and excellent servants and I am going to get married. If my intended husband lets me down I shall open a beauty parlor in Palm Beach. I'm tired of Europe. I have already sent some of my things out there and I have sent money too. Your money is safe with a dictator. He keeps the greedy people down, those who want to nationalize everything and take what isn't theirs to take. Get married again, Lilia; then you will be happy again. It is a new life."

At this Angel squealed. He had slid down under the table, where he saw bits of food and he sat under Dr. Blaise's chair. Dr. Blaise trod on his foot. Bill half rose and cried:

"Angel, come here to your sweetheart. No one meant to hurt you, Angel. Everyone loves Angel. Dr. Blaise loves you, Angel. No one would hurt you purposely. It was all an accident, darling. He meant to stroke you, darling. Sit here, darling, safe behind your sweetheart's back. There!"

She grinned at the doctor. The dog crouched trembling behind her.

A little later, when they had had their liqueurs, the Princess told several stories of how to get black-market funds; then suddenly became bored and said:

"And now Angel must sing. He has waited very patiently."

The doctor burst out laughing. The Princess plumped Angel between herself and Madame Blaise and began to sing in a piping old voice, "D'ye ken John Peel?" which was the song Angel sang, she said.

After a few bars, in fact, Angel opened his mouth and broke into a series of howls reasonably varied and moans reasonably scaled. The maître d'hôtel, who was standing behind a distant service bar, hastily put down a glass he had been rubbing and hurried across the room. The doctor, who was holding his ribs with laughter at the sour faces worn by the rest of the company (except Mrs. Trollope), waved him away, but he stood dubiously in the next booth, now unoccupied. From the booth on the other side came a surprising American woman, five feet ten tall, elegantly and suitably dressed, who had been speaking French all the evening, fluently and with a strong mid-Western accent, and who had been running like a yearling between the telephone and her present friends. She said:

"Oh, quel chien adorable!"

"I hope we didn't disturb you," said Mr. Wilkins, laughing quietly.

"Oh, ne vous en faites pas; I love dogs," said the American woman.

She then called, using her fingers, hands, arms and her long supple body for this, each of her company to look at the adorable dog singing; and she declared that they had had a cat to talk on the radio, but that that cat had died; and that this dog really sang.

"Il chante; on ne peut le nier."

The Princess said at once: "I am going to South America to get married and I must sell Angel to someone who loves him. He has a wonderful pedigree, sire and dam champions for generations. He is so affectionate. You have love and pedigree guaranteed; that is a nice package deal."

The American said: "Oh, I love him. How much is Angel?"

"Two hundred dollars in dollars."

"Oh, it is a lot of dollars. Not that I am sure he isn't worth it. But I am going to South America too. Franco said Switzerland will be the center of the next war. I trust him. I think it is better to go while the going is good."

"So do we," said Mr. Wilkins.

"But the question is where," said Mrs. Trollope.

They discussed it again; and when the American woman had gone back to her table and they were having a second round of coffee, brought in silver pots and ordered by the doctor, Madame Blaise began showing some more photographs—one showed the house owned by herself and the doctor in Basel.

"What a beautiful house," said Mr. Pallintost, thankful that it was no teratological specimen this time.

It was a brick dwelling with three storys and an attic, flat-faced, modern, with a terrace running round the corner of the second story and an awning over it. Round the house was a garden behind iron railings.

Said Mrs. Pallintost: "I cannot understand why you live in a hotel, Madame Blaise."

"When you live in a house there are servants, they have to have orders, I hate giving orders and scolding when they are not obeyed, for they never are. But we have a housekeeper Ermyntrud, who is ugly and old and a spinster, and she loves to do that. At least in the hotel I think about nothing."

The Princess studied the photograph; and said, "But surely, Madame, with such a beautiful home you ought to stay in it and help your husband."

"Oh, I am quite satisfied with her staying in the hotel," said the doctor.

"I shall never go home," said Madame Blaise.

"No, you will never come home," said the doctor grimly.

"He talks about nothing but disease and sickness. I must wait till he comes home for a drink. He locks up the drinks. And when we sit down to dinner he tells me details of every horrible disease he has seen in the hospital and shows me photographs of his patients. He has a cabinet full at home and only I am allowed to see them."

"But you will go home when the next winter is over," said Mr. Pallintost, shocked.

"Oh, no, I'm going to stay here for life."

The doctor said:

"Oh, I don't think she will ever leave here alive. I am glad for her to stay here for life. Marriage is a curse and the more I am free of her the better I feel."

Madame Blaise said seriously: "I am looking for romance and I should go off on my own, only that I must do all the business and money matters for my husband and son and daughter. Without me they would be in rags. I brought all the money to the house. A physician eats up all he earns. I did not wish to have this house but the doctor insisted upon it for his prestige; and I hate it. I always hated that house, it is a prison, a death-house. While I am there, I have a feeling that I shall never get out of it alive."

"The fact is, she sits there all day and never attempts to get out," said the doctor.

"But, Madame, you said you were going to the U.S.A.," said the Princess.

"Oh, yes, we are going to the U.S.A. to look for our son spoiled by her. If he doesn't break his neck first. He will break it one way or another the way she has brought him up."

"What is the use of my house? I built it to please him. He wanted a house in Basel near the Schutzmatt Park and I built it for him and he is afraid to live there because the Germans or the Russians can march into Basel in a minute. At the same time he does not want to transfer his practice to South America or the U.S.A."

The Princess said: "Well, South America is good, there are so many skin diseases. But I met a doctor in New York, a very rich man, a friend of mine, who said nine-tenths of the babies in South America are diseased and should be gassed; he said the atom bomb wouldn't do them the least harm; they should be exterminated. He toured South America and he was shocked.

American science could do nothing for them. He is a splendid husband and father and he has seven children and knows what he is talking about."

Lilia said: "I think that is cruel."

The Princess said: "Oh, science is cruel; and this is a cruel age."

Lilia said: "I call it a very cruel age; I never know where to turn. It is the communists who have driven us so far out of our old ways of thinking, and the blame is on them. I wish we could do to them what they do to others, take them out, stand them up against a wall and shoot them and then we should have some peace. After all, they set the pace; we are all hag-ridden."

Mr. Wilkins said: "Lilia, I think we need a little amusement. Let's go to the Palace Splendide for a dance and a drink."

"Oh, let's go to the Savoy Grand," said the doctor. He and Madame Blaise kept insisting that they should go to the Savoy Grand, and soon the whole party walked in under the elephantine portico, an old-fashioned structure with frowning front on the heights of Lausanne. They passed through various lobbies and a foyer, a long cocktail room and past several bars at which American soldiers from Germany and local young folk were drinking, and pushed their way into a dining room beyond the crowded dance floor, a long high-ceilinged room with a few tables set for drinks for overflow guests, near the glass doors. Lilia said:

"Oh, I hate anything artificial that reminds me of the East. What made the Aga Khan buy a whole block here? Why should he come here at all?"

But the others felt a certain thrill in spite of the miserable accommodation and a rather rude reception, because in this hotel lived several ex-kings. They laughed a little at the protocol difficulties of setting kings around one table, until someone said that each king ate separately in his room or suite to avoid such difficulties. Mrs. Trollope said that she had come not long ago to see a crown prince aged nine and that she had bowed the knee and the prince had kissed her hand; and Madame Blaise mentioned a native prince she had met here. Whereupon Mr. Wilkins said: "But what about us? What about the Archduke who lives in our hotel?"

The Pallintosts opened their eyes at this. Dr. Blaise, smirking, said he had seen the Archduke that very afternoon. The Archduke was a member of the Jury (as he put it) in the Almanach de Gotha, he was in fact the Foreman of the Jury, he was, you might say, Exile Number One, the poorest and All-highest. "And he lives in our hotel?" said Mrs. Trollope.

"The archduke has sixteen quarterings; he represents Hapsburg, Dalberg, Hohenzollern, Wittelsbach, Orange, Lorraine, Anjou-Valois, Guelph-Wettin, Bourbon, Braganza, Vasa, Holstein-Vottorp-Romanov, Savoy, Jagiellon, Aragon, Isauris-Porphyrogenitus. If we had invited that nasty old man Herr Altstadt you met on the stairs and suspected of stealing a one-hundred-franc note, Mrs. Trollope, we should have had this enormous company with us." The doctor laughed immoderately.

The Princess had lost all her vivacity at what she considered the doctor's attack upon her position. "Doctor, how can you remember all that?"

"Anyone who is jealous can remember it; and as I was only made by my wife's money, as she mentioned, I am very jealous, and ironic too. I am a satirist of human nature, of which I have the worst opinion. Aristocracy takes its position by force. There is no quality of any kind in human nature. Human nature is invariably pleased by the feats of thieves, torturers, liars, more than by other qualities and frankly I think the muck-rakers and iconoclasts are absurd. To us murderers and robbers are gods. That is the history behind the Almanach de Gotha, and we creep and crawl before it."

"My goodness, you are a terrible cynic," said Mrs. Pallintost.

"Oh, let's dance, Lilia," said Mr. Wilkins.

"Do you know what it is never to have had any happiness?" said the doctor, grinning strangely at Mrs. Pallintost.

Mrs. Trollope had not heard Mr. Wilkins. She remained in her seat, staring at the doctor with her black eyes wide open, bending forward so that her low-cut black lace dress showed her round breasts, with the skin long tanned and creased by tropic suns.

The waiter brought them the drinks asked for, whisky-and-soda and kummel. Suddenly the "cousins" became different persons. They insisted upon better whisky and greater quantity, they wanted to see the labels. They said it was like old times and they went off to dance together in a pretty coupling, their faces lit up. Anyone could see that they were for a moment back in the East they had had together and that had now gone. Meanwhile, the gloomy Swiss couple drank kummel; and the doctor said:

"I wish we could drop them and go home; I am tired of this farce."

The Princess had gone to the powder room and left Angel tied to her chair.

Ignoring the Pallintosts, Madame Blaise said: "You'll have to pay this time."

"I know, but I managed him well, didn't I? He's not an Englishman of class and he didn't dare countermand my orders."

"Who could have?" said Madame Blaise, laughing.

"I could have if it had been done to me," said the doctor. He leaned back and showed his somewhat rounded belly. "It was a good dinner; it did me good. But the best was the satisfaction I got out of leeching onto the little rubber salesman."

"Let's leech all we can out of the damned ruined robber Empire and lick up the bloodspots. Little salesmen and their half-caste mistresses running here to be safe from doomsday and thinking themselves our equals."

"They are my equals; and doomsday always comes," said the doctor, laughing, with a sidelong glance towards his wife.

Madame Blaise said: "They're rich. Between them, they have about one half of what I have command of: I mean the money in New York—"

"You talk about that too much. People always guess where you got it."

"I got it from Nazis. Where are Nazis now? Dirt, filth, No one worries about that trash. It's mine. Everyone's against Nazis now. Once they were on top of the world and everyone was afraid of them. But it came to us, didn't it; it came to us!"

The doctor made a sour face. "It came to you. What comes to me I have to earn."

"We'll have to invite them back, you know."

The doctor laughed. "Not to the same tune. I'll invite them for the anniversary of the day I met you and we'll give them lentil soup and cornmeal cakes. Isn't that what you're going to leave me?"

"My money's for my son."

"Your son! Your son is a fine specimen. He won't live to get it. I'll get it!" And the doctor made a peculiar gesture, twisting his thumb and finger together and pulling sharply.

"If you live to get it. Perhaps I should do something about that."

"Yes, you're the active one," said the doctor grinning.

The dance floor was crowded. Lilia and Robert circulated and had become graver, once alone. Robert said in a low voice:

."That came a bit steep!"

"The doctor was so rude. I think he's a detestable character. I know why Gliesli lives away from him."

"I really thought he went out of his way to sting me!"

"I am sure he did. I always think he has something up his sleeve. At first I liked him. He seemed so sweet to his wife; you remember, we said how attentive he was, always coming to take care of her, bringing her her medicine. We said, There's a united couple. But now he gives me a cold turn. And he gives her her drugs: he rations her—that's why she's so dependent, when she's so rich."

"Sh! He's an old man who puts on wickedness because he's tired and disappointed and he's tired of her. But their manners are abominable. I hope we never go out with them again."

"But they're sure to invite us back."

"Why must we accept?"

"We live at such close quarters."

"That's the trouble with these little hotels and pensions. You get too close to people's skins."

"You couldn't get too close to Madame Blaise's skin. Do you know, I don't think she ever gets fully undressed."

He shuddered, "Lilia, don't. But surely when he's here—and he's a doctor—"

"Robert! But seriously, poor woman! She has not been near the doctor for over five years. She does not want him to guess that she is no longer a young woman. She says if he ever guesses that she has reached a certain age, he will leave her. And so she pretends to be afraid of catching cold. And then she thinks a bathroom used by other people or even a stair-rail is full of disease. The doctor has scared her. She protects herself by wearing three or four of everything, from the skin out. When she goes to bed she keeps on four suits of underwear, four pairs of wool stockings, she has two flannel nightgowns, a wool jacket, a dressing gown with her head tied up in a shetland wool scarf. She has never taken a bath in the hotel. She keeps her windows locked. She won't go into the hall without her fur coat. She isn't happy with the doctor; and he can't be happy with her."

Robert wagged his head and sighed. Lilia said:

"All through the winter she washes only her face and hands, for fear of colds."

The music ceased and they returned to the table. Madame Blaise was saying to the Princess the things she always said to Lilia:

"Shall I go and see my son? Do you think I can influence him? Shall I take a boat or a plane? What shall I say to my son to influence him? I am going to telegraph my son; what shall I say? How much do you think it costs? What shall I do with my money in the United States? How can I get it back?"

Mrs. Pallintost was talking about some people they knew in Embassy circles.

"My friends did not know quite what to do. They met these Russians and no one was talking to them and they felt, just out of pity, they should say something, and immediately they were invited to the Soviet Embassy. They were warned not to go, it would involve them; but they thought there might be a middle ground; and at the last moment they were told they would be compromised even if they stayed on the middle ground, so they refused and instead sent a Christmas card; and the Russian people sent them a silver rose bowl. They were embarrassed and perhaps it was intended that they should feel embarrassed. My friends did not know what to do, but they compromised since they could not do nothing, by sending the Russians a pound of tea. You know Russians are immensely fond of tea."

"Well, I think that was rather nice," said Lilia.

"Yes, but they have probably involved themselves."

"Oh, but how?"

"Oh, you know they have card indexes on everyone. But the chief thing was, they heard from the servants of people who knew servants of the Russian Embassy—"

"Oh, so they have servants!"

"Well, it was a governess there—"

"Oh, so they have governesses too."

"She told them the complete agenda, how everything is to be done. Switzerland a focus, France to be invaded—"

"Oh, Robert, what do you think of that? It's true, for she heard it from this friend in the Diplomatic Service."

Robert smirked. Having been on the commercial side all his life, he thought little of career diplomats. "Embassy servants don't get that kind of news."

Madame Blaise said: "I think they know what's going on. At any rate I'm flying out to advise my son."

The band was tuning up. The Princess sang "John Peel" and Angel with her. Some people looked at them but the dancers were getting in their last dances. Most night spots in Switzerland close at twelve and it was almost twelve.

On the drive home, through the silent well-lighted mist-filled streets and the country roads along walled gardens with mighty old trees, the Pallintosts following them in their little car, the headlights swinging along and around, they all felt pleasant; and for some reason the doctor offered to take Angel home with him to Basel when he went on Monday morning early. They would sell Angel to someone who would take him without a pedigree and the Princess was to get the pedigree eventually. The Princess was very happy.

They had to stop first at the Hotel Lake Terrace, a little hotel higher up the hill, where the Princess had just gone. Since the dog occupied a bed, the Hotel Swiss-Touring was charging the Princess double, not to mention the price for extra laundry. The Hotel Lake Terrace, almost empty, had agreed to take her and the dog for less. Mrs. Trollope felt nervous. When they stopped in front of the Lake Terrace, she said she would go up for a little talk with the Princess.

"Oh, do come home," said Mr. Wilkins; but Mrs. Trollope responded sharply and drily.

When they reached the Swiss-Touring, Mrs. Pallintost and Madame Blaise went upstairs together. Mr. Wilkins said: "Would you care to take a little walk? I thought the air in Lausanne fresh, but here it is like wine, it is full of ozone."

The doctor said he was going to bed. Mr. Pallintost said he always liked to walk before sleeping. He and Mr. Wilkins took a few turns along several hundred yards of the lakeside promenade. They went through the park and approached the landing for the Evian boat. The lake was misty. Mr. Wilkins said:

"It is quite romantic here when the moon is out. You look opposite and you would say the mountains of the moon."

"I understand you're going to Basel to visit your friends the Blaises? You might like to drive there in your own car."

"Dr. Blaise has not mentioned that," said Mr. Wilkins.

"Your cousin was saying she might visit Basel to see Madame Blaise's house. It seems Madame Blaise is thinking of returning home for a short visit."

There was a brief pause. Mr. Wilkins cleared his throat and said, in a delightful voice, "Yes, yes, she might do that. You see it is my cousin who is buying the car for me. She wants to make me a little present. She has extra Swiss francs lying about. We may as well see a bit of the country while we are here. We do not know where we shall be next year—we thought of the Côte d'Azur, Casablanca, South America."

"Ah? Why not go to the States? You can make money there."

"You can make money anywhere."

But Mr. Wilkins became thoughtful. At last he said quietly: "Lilia says you would not recognize me now, if you knew me some years ago. That is the result of retirement, Mr. Pallintost, I am not the same man. I think of getting back into some small business; but I need heat, as much of it as there is going, don't you see, and we thought of Casablanca. But there must be something to stop me from sleeping all the time. All I do is take a little walk, not to feel liverish. But you know I often do feel liverish. We dine at seven-thirty. Usually we go straight up and go to bed early. I wake early, for it's the only time you can get anything done in the East and I have the habit."

After another pause he said: "I am trying to get my cousin to bring out all her pounds, but she doesn't see it."

"Doesn't your cousin—uh, Mrs. Trollope, believe in the Swiss franc?"

"Oh, rather," said Mr. Wilkins and again fell silent.

Mr. Pallintost said hesitatingly: "My wife and I feel we must thank you for the evening we had, you know. You were very generous. My wife and I don't go in much for high living, but we thought the cooking excellent and we enjoyed the wine; though we take so little in general, we are not very good judges."

"Mrs. Trollope and I rarely take it."

"But this—it is the Johannisberger the doctor is so fond of—I preferred the Dambacher you know. I think I might get to like that too much perhaps. Le vice du pays, eh? Ha!" said Mr. Pallintost, hinting.

"H'm," said Mr. Wilkins, not wishing to comment then upon the doctor's ways. He continued at last: "I'm quite a comic; just a little wine or none at all. I haven't the habit. Everything is habit, I suppose."

The bells began to ring midnight. Mr. Wilkins, in his clear light baritone with its Yorkshire guttural at moments, continued:

"As for South America, all I've seen of it is in Walt Disney. I hear there are opportunities in Bogota though."

"Euh—h'm" said Mr. Pallintost.

"The air is so thick I shall sleep like a dormouse," said Mr. Wilkins.

"I think the ladies will be wondering if we have taken a swim."

"A bit early in the year for that, eh? But I have not seen Lilia come back from the Hotel Lake Terrace. I do wish she would not stay up so late talking to the Princess: the Princess is quite a comic. A great converter. And the next day, you know, Lilia always says she has a backache; and I have more fun than a cartload of monkeys getting doctors from all over town."

They dragged another turn or two, when Lilia was seen trotting out of the entrance of the Lake Terrace. Mr. Wilkins made a few terse stately reproaches and they all went in. Lilia was even more nervous than before, and when Mr. Wilkins had said good night she shut her door and went to bed herself; but to toss about and remember each word she had said to the Princess and the Princess to her.

Brought to light and analyzed, the unexpected injustice, the ugliness of the thing upset her. Bili was so very decided, she was already in campaign: "You won't stop me, Lilia dear. The man must be brought to his senses."

Bili—strange old hummingbird, lively, colored, clever, with her flesh in folds and pouches from too much dieting, tapping and scurrying along like a girl, decided, foolish, coquettish, dashing—was not Lilia's ideal friend. But she was lavish, devoted and what she said was common sense.

"He has had your loyalty and devotion for twenty-seven years."

"Never another man, Bili, only my husband and then Robert. I never even thought of another man. I was so sure he would marry me the year we came abroad. I came abroad with him without a thought. What a scandal! But I didn't even think of it. I thought Mr. Trollope was a rotter, a gadabout; but he behaved very handsomely at the last; and Robert does not measure up to him. I have few kind words to say for my husband, but in this he was everything a gentleman should be."

She had not wept then with the Princess; but spoke briskly, harshly, sadly. She had been brought up in a convent of French nuns in the East, gone home to England and returned to marry Mr. Trollope.

"I feel as if I am being punished now, Bili, in Madeleine."

Madeleine was the younger of Mrs. Trollope's two daughters. She had been engaged several times; once had turned the man down on her wedding eve. She was dazzling, with the fresh beauty of blood newly mixed; Mrs. Trollope's mother had been a Dutch-Javanese.

"Madeleine has that Javanese walk," said Mrs. Trollope.

This was supposed to be a secret, though the Dutch never

cared about mixed blood. Eventually Mrs. Trollope told everything to everyone; she was not used to being despised and hated. She had lived in the unreal world of empire outposts for many years and in fashionable places abroad. She had been protected by the gallant rascality of Mr. Trollope and the gallant loyalty of Mr. Wilkins. With the departure of the gallant rascal, the gallant Mr. Wilkins had shown a poorer side.

"Everyone likes Robert at first sight. It is only much later you find out that he has a heart of stone. It is not his fault but the fault of his whole family. No one counts but the Wilkinses and their blood must not be mixed with a half caste. That is what they call me. It does not even matter if there are no more Wilkinses, they are so precious. Someone wrote a letter to the old mother saying that my last child, Thomas, called after Mr. Trollope, was really Robert's child. His old mother had a heart attack and called him back to Yorkshire. I must say that Robert did not go; or not until it suited him. That is quite characteristic of the Wilkinses: they do what suits them and that is what God thinks right. They would not give you a cup of water if you were dying in the gutter, Princess, and they knew you were a Princess. They do not care about Princess or Queen or God Almighty. They would only give a cup of water to a Wilkins, and then only if it suited them. The world has been hard to them, taken no notice of them, made them soulless commonplace people; in their stiff vanity they resent it, they secretly know what they are and they would like to see us all die before them. Their selfish mother tried to make them all old maids and they hate a woman like me, Bili. And through defending them he has become like them: he is one of them. And now Robert has quarreled with them bitterly; and he does not care at all. I assure you he would quarrel with me, without a flicker of feeling, without batting an eyelash, if it were not for my money. Oh, yes, I have brought abroad £8,000 and I have a lot still to bring, and that is the basis of Robert's loyalty."

She had said all that to the Princess. It had all come direct, tabloid from her, because she had thought it over so many times. She had already told some of it to a good many people, trying to explain the shame and disgrace of her life. She had not mentioned his habit of not talking to her at table. She was deeply ashamed that these petty things bothered her. She was ashamed when she compared her dreamed life of true love, happiness, hope and trust with the insignificance of her present life.

But Bili had wanted none of this.

"You shan't suffer, Lilia. We will jab him out of his lethargy, physical and moral. We must begin tomorrow. I am coming down to breakfast with you; I shall come to lunch too and to dinner. He will get no peace from me. You need someone who is relentless. He is a weak man. You must give him no peace."

"Oh, Bili, how can I nag him on such a subject? I can't do it."

"You can't but I can and I will."

"Oh, Bili, not at table; I won't know where to look."

"Do as you please, Lilia. But this must be settled now; he is getting lazier and lazier and he is getting to have less and less regard for your feelings. What is more, Lilia, you must refuse to bring out any more of your money until he marries you."

"How could I bring pressure to bear on him like that? With money? Oh, Bili, if you knew how we felt for each other in the East—it was love, there was such a bond. That bond must still be there. I know it is. I know if I went away, he would be miserable: he cannot live without me. It's a life bond. How can I be straight and cold with a man who has that relation to me?"

"Yes, you're no use as a negotiator. You must let me handle it. And I will, but when I ask you to, you must arrange for me to have lunch with Robert alone."

At the memory of this terrible hour with the Princess, Lilia wept and her face burned. She said now to herself:

"Oh, Bili, I would rather leave him; though it would be suffering for us both, rather than take such measures with a man I love and have loved so much for so long."

Mrs. Trollope tossed all through the night. She was afraid of what would happen tomorrow.

The afternoon before there had been the usual upheaval, sweeping and polishing between guests; and early in the morning there was a noisy movement and a strong resonant English voice had begun to blow on the landing upstairs, relating some pension story of tipping and service; the old old story of the unhappy hotel dwellers; and after this story, which boomed through the half-waking hotel, the great voice, the voice of an old sea officer calling down the decks in an early morning fog, said:

"Thank you very very much; I am very very grateful."

It was the Admiral; she had returned.

Her voice was answered by a greasy persuasive voice, without timber, the voice of kindness, the voice of the poor helper, the unwilling travel acquaintance, and this voice said:

"Now lie down, rest, you had all this fuss and bother, now lie down, it is nearly breakfast time; you will get your cup of tea."

The great voice shouted:

"No, thank you very very much. You go back and have yours. I am having mine at the table. Thank you very much. I am very very grateful. Come and see me one of these days—not tomorrow. I am going to see the Edward G. Robinson picture and then going out; but come one of these days."

The door shut, and the helpers—there were two, a middle-aged couple in the ill-fitting, drab and numerous garments the poor English tripper wears—went down the stairs together holding hands.

Mrs. Trollope, who was already dressed, thought she would go upstairs to welcome the Admiral and so distract her mind from her own troubles. She went up to the next floor. There was silence. But suddenly there was a stirring, and she was startled by a mighty squawk, "Awkh-aw-wkh! Oh-aw-kh! Eh?" Silence. She waited. A moment later there was a slight movement, a sound like a giant yawning in a limestone cavern, distant and near and echoing, "Aw-wh-awh-awh!" An explosive, sonorous, overpowering and resounding yawn followed it, awesome, disturbing, "Aw-aw-awkh-ah-ah-awkh!" It was the strength that was awesome, for it was a woman in spite of the baritone, and it was sane, capable. It seemed like some limitless being who, for a reason obscure, had taken on the flesh of a superannuated tea-drinking English paying guest. Mrs. Trollope retreated, but kept her door open. Then there was a mild roaring in the room upstairs, the lift went down and up, and tea was brought; and then Mrs. Trollope, thinking she might perhaps now talk to the poor old lady, alone in the world at eighty-seven, went up again.

There was silence, then a complacent, clanking "Aw-whk-awkh-eh-eh!" Then silence. Mrs. Trollope hesitated. It seemed to her she heard her sparrows complaining on her windowsill. The sun was shining in the back of the hotel. "Aw-whk-whsk-eh!" There was a bird somewhere with a musical note. The breakfast bell rang. The voice said:

"Well, goodbye, little Caroline; don't be lonely, little Caroline."

Mrs. Trollope feared a familiar spirit. But a canary tweeked in the room, so Mrs. Trollope made haste and went below. A scene took place on the upstairs landing; something was wrong. The old lady's ungainly French clanked along. Mrs. Trollope heard, Luisa heard, then Charlie, then Clara. I went to the door of my office and listened but did not go up. I had taken the old woman back, because she had had trouble at the Lake Terrace and I still had empty rooms. I thought I would give her another chance and I was going to warn the servants about their frolics; fair is fair. The Admiral croaked:

"Je veux voir Madame. Est-ce Madame ou Mamzell? Dites-lui qu'il faut qu'elle vienne."

They all began to argue. Bells rang. "Clara, venez ici!" The Admiral liked Clara, fortunately. A stick tapped. The door opened and shut. "Awkh!" After a silence, a canary answered, "Twee-eek!" "My little Caroline, my little friend." "Twee-eek!" "Goodbye, Caroline, my little friend." The door opened and shut; then the terror came. The stick—tap-tap-tap. The voice, "Clara, vous êtes mon amie, venez-ici." Clara's spattering French: she had to go to the kitchen. Then: "Eh! L'homme qui est là! L'homme! Où est l'homme? Où est-il, l'homme?"

Grinning, Charlie limped upstairs. "What is your name?"

"Charles."

She spoke in English: "Charles, why doesn't the lift work now? It wasn't worth my trouble to come back here and find the lift still doesn't work."

"It does work but it's being painted. See the notices."

"If it works bring it down for me. I don't care about notices."

"We're not allowed, Madame."

"Eh? Ring it down. Eh? L'homme! Monsieur le peintre! Eh? Bring it down! Get Madame, get Madame at once."

There was a sort of public meeting on the landing. Clara ran up and downstairs.

"No, such things don't exist, such things are impossible," said she.

"Clara, you are my friend. Everything is possible. Get the painter out of the lift. What does he want it for? Go and get it, Clara."

Running on the stairs.

"Go and get it, l'homme."

Running on the stairs. She thundered with her stick. She was deserted. Breakfast was on and they had flown in all directions. She rattled with her stick, the poor old bully in a great rage, in misery; for she suffered from rheumatism and she cried out, she cried in desperation to herself:

"I am mad to come back here, je suis folle de revenir ici, I am mad to come here, why did I come?"

Mrs. Trollope was very much upset by the Admiral's predicament. There was silence and she thought she had gone away, given up, gone to her room; but no, she was standing there all the time, formidable, irreducible, miserable in the strength that can't be turned off or controlled, unable to walk down, too proud to return to her room, deserted in her painful age.

"After all I have a right to have my breakfast."

She called again to the painter, the man. Silence. What was to happen? Mrs. Trollope was torn. Should she go up and reason with the old lady, help her down? Or ask "Madame"? No. Two persons had returned, were standing arguing, whispering outside Mrs. Trollope's room; then they softly climbed the stairs and consoled, promised. Just then there was a sound like a not-yet-heard wind. It rattled a little like the beginning of a wind against the shutters at night, without snow or rain. It was the electric motor of the new lift. It glided down, came to a stop. The Admiral said "Ah-ah-ah," in a long sigh.

The painter took her down to the dining room. Charlie the porter stopped next to Mrs. Trollope on the stairs and said to Clara who was below:

"I am this minute telephoning Le Bon Dieu to influence her to go." And indeed at this moment everyone, including Mrs. Trollope, was hoping the poor old woman would go; but where? She had fled from the Labor Government; Mrs. Trollope knew she had no reason for this, and the whole thing made her sad; she felt more homeless than before.

Mr. Wilkins was having his breakfast and reading the paper. Mrs. Trollope looked in the mirror and saw all that was happening. There was a gay high-colored French-Swiss mother with her daughter, a good-looking nervous girl of about twenty-five. Before each meal they went shopping and brought to the table a shopping bag of vegetables. Gennaro or another brought in a pail of water, which he placed beside the table, and a basin of water, which he put on a chair beside. At the beginning of each meal the couple arrived and, standing at the table, began vigorously scrubbing, washing, rinsing and grating carrots and celery, which they ate with various uncooked leaf vegetables. A screen was placed behind their table, and the mother, while at work, looked round the room at the diners with a smiling, inviting vanity, while the daughter, embarrassed, stood with her back to the room. With the flushed mother and daughter, the red screen, the strange emotions, the table, chairs, pail and basin, the heap of vegetables, it was like a play from a distant country, performed every lunch and dinner.

Mr. Wilkins said: "There is a vegetarian pension in town; why doesn't she go there?"

Mrs. Trollope said: "But perhaps they did not agree with those vegetarians; possibly they had theories of their own."

The mother was thin, flushed, pleased; they spoke to no-one. Mr. Wilkins was addressing Mrs. Trollope:

"One time in the Raffles Hotel I met a chap from Poona who had a wife, a delicious creature—"

"Oh, yes, you mean Mrs. Cibolles—"

"Don't interrupt, Lilia; yes, Cibolles. His brother owned property in Adelaide, Australia, and he swore it was going to develop amazingly; and you remember they introduced us to a man who used to be in French West Africa."

"Oh, I went to the races with that man and won three times on three horses called Jehosaphat, Hosea and Hosanna, all from the same stables; that is why I picked them. And he, his name was Vidal, he had the form sheets and did not win once."

"Lilia, I do wish you would not interrupt. As I was saying, they gave me an introduction to a fellow from Poona who had been in gunnies you know, in Calcutta. I knew him for years and years and he said to me, 'I am through with India; all the business is passing into the hands of Indians.' That is where the British Empire is now. Time to quit and I quit in time."

Their behavior was marital. It was incomprehensible to everyone why Mr. Wilkins pretended still that they were acquaintances, cousins, traveling together. Tears came into her eyes, but she did not let him see them.

"I must bear my troubles alone and I am not alone. Nothing can break the bond between us; but he amuses himself pretending it is not there. I am not going to ask why. The Church does not tell me, my saint does not tell me; and the Princess is right, something must be done. But I can't do it."

She said aloud; "Robert, I am going upstairs. I don't feel well."

"You need exercise."

"What exercise do you do but walk? And my legs are short; I cannot walk so far. Perhaps I won't see you for lunch."

"You must do as you please. My mother always said, Those who do not wish to eat must not be forced to. Those who are hungry will eat."

She had not done her crossword puzzle last night and so had not slept as well. Sometimes, in the middle of the dark hours, about three-thirty or four, she would suddenly wake and think of a word she had not been able to find. It gave her pleasure. It was a fact that, since she had started this intellectual work at night, she had done better. But some nights it did not work. She would hear, on one side, Mr. Wilkins deeply asleep, since eleven, and on the other, the sleep mutterings of that strange cocoon, Madame Blaise, wrapped in her stifling room, her blankets, dressing jacket and all the rest. Where was there anyone slightly normal, jolly, busy, such as Lilia had known in the old days? Then she had had many real friends.

Lilia slipped out of the hotel and took a walk by herself.

"I shall take something in that other tearoom where no one I know goes. I cannot go to lunch. I am to have tea at four o'clock with Bili. I am not going down to lunch to face some page of *The Times* or *Financial Times* and see all that is going on in the mirror."

At lunch she heard Gliesli making the noises preparatory to going down and she was not surprised to see her coming through the intermediate door.

"Liliali, come down, dear, for lunch; you know you are hungry."

She was hungry, even for the thin potato soup the German cook had prepared; the new French cook had not come yet. Madame Blaise, as usual, was dressed for lunch, in her old brown hat, trimmed with a fur band, her fur coat, her brown wool dress, her gloves and handbag, with new fur boots, rather pretty, halfway up her calves.

"Gliesli dear, I am not going; I am too unhappy. I am most unhappy. Go down. I cannot face another meal with Robert reading the paper and myself looking in that big mirror. I can see everything that everyone does; and it all has nothing to do with me. I can see Mrs. Powell making a big half-circle to avoid saying good day to me."

"Why should she? Don't be foolish, Lilia; I need you. I have promised to go back to Basel and I am very worried. I am going to die there."

"Gliesli, Mrs. Powell avoids me because she is a selfish stiff-necked old woman. She knows I am not married to Robert. She knows because she asked the servants; or Madame Bonnard told her. We have no friends, Gliesli, do you realize that? You and I have no real friends in the world but each other. You have a son and daughter, I have three children; but they are leading their own lives, their love has turned away from us. We are on the shelf. It is not their fault. The world is hard: life has taught them to be hard. And apart from that, I cannot face Robert again. My heart has turned against him. I am not angry with him; there is something here," she said, pressing her heart, "which would never allow me to do that. But now I must leave him. For so many years I depended upon him. My own children loved him. Now it is all in the open. My children say, Where is your honor? I never thought of honor when I thought of Robert. I thought only of Robert. But now I can see he does not think of me. I tell him, 'I am suffering,' and he says: 'What sufferings have you? I am looking after your money: our old age is taken care of.' I suppose I made a great mistake; but I know I would make the same mistake again. What can I do, Gliesli? He told me he loved me; he did love me. I loved him. I am glad, whatever happens, that I had that; it is real. It would have been hard if I had never had that love. Everything almost melts away, when I remember that. Often before this I meant to go away and I couldn't. But now I cannot go down and face him reading the *Financial Times*. If he loves me, Gliesli, why must he say, 'She is not my wife but my cousin?' when no one cares at all? Before, there was always the excuse that my husband would not allow us to marry; but my husband allowed it. Why is it? Is it for his own pride? Is it—no, no. He is not like Mrs. Powell. He was a very good businessman. Everyone respected him; perhaps they didn't all like him. But I was so glad of him, so infatuated, I thought they were wrong. I was so happy; but then it made me happy to be with him. When it is too late, you find out he has no heart at all: he is selfish, cold, lazy. I laid my head all these years on a stone. I cannot go down and hear him say, when he lays down the paper, 'You see, Lilia, how right I am when I want you to transfer your money'; and Gliesli, because he can work on my feelings and I have no plans, he is slowly engulfing all my money. Ah, Gliesli—it has broken my heart. In the end, Mr. Trollope was my only friend, but only when he left me. Oh, Gliesli, my heart is crumbling; there is nothing there. It would be more honest to die than to go through this; well, I won't go through it. I don't know what I will do. I am not going down, Gliesli, to see Robert taking his two soups behind his newspaper, while I watch this sad lot of scarecrows that we are, in the mirror."

Madame Blaise said: "Well, my dear, I must go down. I am hungry. If I don't go now, that detestable little peasant whore will find some excuse for bringing me cold soup with her thumb in it and I don't feel like a scene today. The doctor gave me my medicine. Why don't you take it too, Liliali? You would not have the blues."

"You know I will never take those things," said Mrs. Trollope.

"Why don't you and Mr. Wilkins come home with me to Basel and see what my husband is doing and what Basel is like, such a hell-spot of trolls, and my husband is one. I must go; my husband will not bring me any more medicine here, so he has got me back. I don't know what he wants me for; to kill me, I suppose. If you were there, he would not dare; or else you could see what happened and be my witness. Oh, but never mind, I shall give him a nice chunk to swallow at the end. Oh—ho; for I'm sure he's sleeping with that ugly old creature, my servant Ermyntrud."

"Oh, hush, Gliesli!"

She could hear Madame Blaise's laughter all the way down the stairs.

Robert brought her up nothing from lunch; he did not inquire after her health. He merely mentioned that Mr. Pallintost seemed anxious to know about the car, and before he went to sleep he said irritably (for she had demurred):

"Lilia, do please go and see that woman who is knocking on the wall."

Mrs. Trollope went in. The previous afternoon, Miss Chillard had gone out for a short ride in a car brought by her friends, to La Tour de Peilz. During her absence, Roger had done an incorrect thing, but one which he was forced to by her debts. He had gone in, opened her cases and found a good deal of money in them; enough to pay her bills. When Miss Chillard returned, about seven, and asked for her supper, he took it to her himself and told her what he knew: that she had the money to pay, She was indignant that her room had been entered and that he had counted her money; she threatened to call the Consul and the police. She now explained again to Mrs. Trollope, asking her to call the Consul.

"Make him listen; I know he is easy-going and does not want trouble. Shake him up. That money is for the doctors. I am going to Zermatt if I can. That is the only place where I am happy and there is only one man who understands me and makes me want to live and he is a doctor there. If I cannot pay him I cannot go, and if I cannot go back to Zermatt why should I

116

live? I am dying now; why do they grudge me a few more months?"

But Roger had said he would insist upon her paying, he had to live too: he had to pay ten percent of the gross every day to the previous owner, those were the difficult conditions under which we had got the hotel; and it was hard to live in winter; few skiers came to the town. If Miss Chillard did not pay, he would send for the Consul and also for the police.

"To a woman in my condition," said the unfortunate woman to Mrs. Trollope.

Mrs. Trollope said she had an appointment for the afternoon, but she would come back to see the invalid in the evening.

"I shall be in jail by then. I did not know the Swiss could be so cruel. The English have always been their friends and kept them going: where would they be without our custom?" asked the sick woman, from the depths of her pillows. She was more cadaverous than ever. She had not eaten anything since the day before. Mrs. Trollope said she would bring her something appetizing to eat; but she must go now.

What she did was to go into Robert and say that she must have the money in the safe. "I am going to buy you that car, Robert, and I am not going to bring out any more money till you deliver that parcel to me. I need the money in the safe for the car. I cannot think what possessed you, an honorable man or so I have known you, to put my money in the safe in your name."

"You know it was to prevent your spending it foolishly. I am here to safeguard you."

"Very well. I accept that. But give it to me now. I am going to see the Princess, and she and I will go and look at cars. If you do not, Robert, I will not buy the car, for I will not believe any more in your bona fides."

To his astonishment, she insisted; and he did in the end come downstairs with her, the safe was opened and he gave her the money. He asked her for a receipt, but she refused: "Why ever should I give a receipt for my own money?"

"Well, I hope you will not be foolish, Lilia. It is my money too."

At this she flushed, said, "I am late already," and went out. Mr. Wilkins went upstairs, his lips moved slightly. he had begun to talk under his breath.

Mrs. Trollope had some business to do. She rarely went out alone. Although she spoke French well enough and the shop people mostly spoke good English, she did not feel grand enough, she felt she was just an ordinary little woman. When she was with Bili she always called her "Princess" before the shop people; when she was with Madame Blaise she felt confident, because Madame Blaise stood no nonsense. She went shopping sometimes with someone else, an Englishwoman whom she had known for a year, who stayed in the Pension Evian, a poor place. This woman, Mrs. Elliott, spoke excellent French; she wore an old tweed coat and no hat on her graying hair. When out with Mrs. Elliott, Mrs. Trollope was able to pretend that she spoke no French and she would say grandly, "Mrs. Elliott, ask them if it will shrink when washed." Women had done this to Mrs. Trollope when she was waiting for her money to come from England. This afternoon, indeed, she had made an arrangement to meet Mrs. Elliott in front of the Splendid Palace in the Place St. François; but as she went up the street it occurred to her that it would not do to let Mrs. Elliott see how rich she was. She intended, in fact, to buy Robert a gold cigarette case which she must leave to have engraved; and the Princess had asked her to get a small cut-glass scent bottle for her handbag. Mrs. Trollope decided to go up by a sidestreet, not to meet her poor friend, and to let the Princess make her own purchase. But Mrs. Elliott had extraordinarily good sight. She saw her from the other end of the Place St. François and came hurrying to her, waving her hand. Mrs. Trollope pretended not to see her and turned into a jeweler's. Mrs. Elliott was still quite distant, but marked where she turned in, and came into the shop too. It is true, Mrs. Trollope had foolishly said, "I want you to help me choose a present."

Mrs. Trollope waved the cigarette cases away as soon as her friend entered and began to question the jeweler about movements for watches. After a lot of talk, she went out without anything; but she could see the jeweler understood well enough; he was used to these ladies.

She then walked straight back home, saying she had a tea appointment, leaving Mrs. Elliott at her pension, with a very deflated expression. So she came back with her purse full, having spent nothing. Because of this, she began to feel grudging. Why should I buy him the cigarette case when he also expects a car from me? I am wrong to give him his every whim. I can't be carping and mean with Robert; and that is my mistake. What shall I do? I would rather leave him than quarrel and carp. If I give him the cigarette case, at which he has hinted several times, he will be quite self-satisfied and think he has me underfoot. He does not believe I am dissatisfied. "Why worry about our future life?" he says; "I am your future life." That is enough for him. I must get away. It will be agony; but this is agony and I am living a life of shame as well. I would rather give the money to a beggar in the street, to poor old Charlie, to Clara, to Luisa, than to Robert who will take it without gratitude, because it is his. She was so upset that she did not notice how she was hurrying, and she reached the lower part of the hill long before teatime: it was too early to go to the Princess. She walked down to the lakeside and sat down on a seat. Sparrows came round her feet; she had no bread for them. "I am sorry, I did not think of you," she said to them.

She was tired and trembling. Suddenly she thought of Miss Chillard. Supposing she, Lilia, did what Robert wanted, brought out all her money, supposing she were left helpless— he was capable of that. Supposing she ended up like that, with her little aches and pains, in a narrow poor hotel room, despised and harassed? She began to pant as if someone were after her. How foolish she had been! Thank goodness it was not yet too late. She had a terrible choice to make, to choose between Robert and some sort of freedom, between a wandering old age and that homeland in which she was a stranger. She felt she must get away to see how it looked from a distance.

"I will go with Gliesli. I cannot stay and face the music, as Bili wants me to do."

And if she married Robert? She would be worse off perhaps. He was married to his family; she would always come second. She saw quite sharply another life in England, where she would be a welcome rich divorcee of good reputation and friendly ways, who would have many friends. She would live in Knightsbridge, get up not too early, have a little maid to come in, trot round the pleasant shopping streets and the park, find friends in bars where her sort collected, go to the races sometimes, be welcome with her children and grandchildren, a sensible sophisticated loving grandmother, taking gifts, buying a French dress, going to dances in hotels. She was fifty, but there were decent men of fifty. Her heart sank; but she and Robert loved each other: "We are one flesh," she had said to him, with deep emotion.

"And one fortune," he said quickly, embarrassed.

"It is only too true. What on earth am I to do? My love is wasted," she said to herself, now, remembering the past.

She started to walk again. She became very tired. Some church or railway clock in the wooded, gardened slopes above her struck a late quarter. She began to hurry up the hill again. When she got to the tearoom, she was red and her hair loose about her face; in a glass she saw that her eyes looked old. The orchestra which began at four had struck the first notes and she heard Angel singing. She saw the Princess at their favorite table. It was a table in a cushioned corner by some large plate-glass windows and looked out on a lawn with exotic trees from hot countries. Many trees here were evergreens from China and the Pacific; some she recognized. They made her heart ache. On the table was a plate of cakes chosen for her and Angel by the Princess. When she reached the Princess, her eyes were dusty and shedding tears.

"Oh, dear Bili, how thankful I am to see you. You do not know how wonderful it is."

She told Bili that things had never been worse: Robert was breaking her heart and did not even feel it. He was estranged and selfish. "You would never recognize that man; he was different in Malaya."

"You see, he is sure of you. You have given him everything. He does not trouble his head."

"Dear Bili, I have left him three times, never telling him, never expecting to come back, and he does not know this; and yet he does write me such faithful letters and says he is lonely, that he has nothing to live for but me; and that is true. Then he telephones to me; he, so careful of expenses, sends me reply-paid telegrams, and my return ticket and he loosens up and sends me presents of cash. To leave a man you must have a reason. He is very clever about that: he has given me no reason. He has never even taken another woman out for a meal. And then, Bili, how can I forget he loved me?"

Said the Princess: "This will never do. Sing, Angel, one more song, and then you will get another cake."

As soon as the orchestra began again, Angel was induced to sing; at the end of the song, in his emotion, he wetted the cushion and then got another cake. The hostess hovered near.

"Lilia, I have fully made up my mind to speak to that man."

Lilia begged her not to do so. "I shall have to leave town."

The Princess was determined. She sat in the full afternoon light and spoke vigorously, nodding her curls, the pink and blue feathers in her pink hat. She wore a low neck and had sleeves halfway up her wasted forearms. Her bust was tightly supported and she had a belt of rough-cut turquoise and silver round her slender waist. She had charm bracelets and jeweled bracelets on each wrist; and high-lacing blue suede buskins with high heels. She looked very very old and very strange. Mrs. Trollope, listening to her, wondered if she were really only the forty-five she pretended to be. Mr. Wilkins said she was in her sixties. But Lilia had seen many wasted worn women in the East.

"I don't believe you have ever shown any character, Lilia."

"It's not in my nature; I am too affectionate, Bili."

"I am going to invite him for lunch; but first have a little talk with him and be straight, tell him how you feel."

"He knows and doesn't care."

"Now you have started this, you cannot stop. Leave it to Bili. Bili gets what she wants. Will you have lunch with me tomorrow at the Lake Club. Just you and Robert and Angel and me."

Mrs. Trollope accepted without saying what was troubling her. The Princess detested Dr. and Madame Blaise. How could she say she contemplated going to stay with them to bring Robert to his senses? She heard the Princess saying that she would arrange the marriage within four months.

"I have married so many people and I am going to get married again myself, at the end of the year, as soon as I have been to the Paris clinic."

Mrs. Trollope, indeed the whole hotel, surmised that the Princess was going in for a face-lift.

"Oh Bili, have you someone in mind?"

"Yes, a young man; he is a young Spaniard and will just suit me. He is not a child: he is thirty-three. We are going out to Buenos Aires and are going to open a restaurant there."

Mrs. Trollope said slowly: "You see, Bili, I do not know if he will do it. Under the export of capital scheme, we get say one thousand pounds each if we are separate and only one thousand pounds altogether if we are married; that is not quite enough for Robert. He knows my money, except for some arrangements made for my children, some trust funds, is to go to him if I predecease him, and, if not, then all to my children."

"You are mad, simply mad. You told that man that you have left all your money to him? Already. Before you're married?"

"But what difference does it make? Bili, he is slowly swallowing it all anyway. His appetite grows and grows. He made about sixty thousand pounds in Malaya and now that he is not in business he wants to make money out of me. And my children are being estranged. My son Claude, as you know, is a grammar-school headmaster, with three children of his own. My daughter-in-law is a fine girl, not pretty but well-educated, and she likes me; but he is turning her against me. My married daughter, Jessamine, has refused to write to me again until I have made Robert see reason, as she puts it. They have formed a plot. I think it was begun by Madeleine. No one is to write to me until I have brought Robert to his senses. This all happened after I told them I had arranged the trust funds. How oddly people behave! Where is love in all this, Bili? I do not know where love is."

"Supposing I write to them, to one of them, and explain things?"

"Oh, Bili, very well. I wish someone would take it all into their hands and solve it for me; it is too much for me."

"Yes, I will arrange everything. And it will all come out all right. And another thing, we must work out how to get your money back into your own hands. How is it he has got it?"

"He has an irrevocable power of attorney; you can get that in Switzerland between foreigners."

"I shall ask a lawyer."

"I did as you suggested, Bili. I got the money out of the safe to buy him the car."

"Are you going to do that?"

"No, Bili—"

"He will ask you and you will say yes."

"No, Bili, no. I prefer to give it away. Bili, I promised to go to Basel, to stay with Madame Blaise for a while. I could write to Robert from there."

To her surprise, the Princess was pleased. If Lilia went to Basel, then the Princess would allow Angel to go with her; and they might find a purchaser, a dog lover, in Basel.

Mrs. Trollope wiped her eyes; the Princess kissed Angel many times, assuring him that she loved him; and they left the tearoom. They went looking for various trinkets in the jewelers' stores; but Bili would not allow Mrs. Trollope to buy the gold cigarette case.

"He expects it, Bili."

"All the better."

She did not get back in time to feed the sparrows; but Robert was waiting with the drinks.

"Robert, the Princess is taking us to the Toucan this evening, if you wish."

"If she will leave the Angel at home."

"Oh, she said she would. But the thing that bothers me is that Dr. and Madame Blaise will hear about it and be very much hurt."

"Why on earth should the Princess include them in her invitation?"

They had a pleasant evening with the Princess, who was generous and gay. Some time in the evening Mrs. Trollope managed to caution the Princess:

"Oh, Bili be careful. I would not cause pain."

When they dropped the Princess at her hotel, she whispered:

"Bili, oh, do not ever mention to Robert what I told you. He would be very much put out and I should be unhappier than ever."

"I am not interested in gossip; I do things," said the Princess.

When the "cousins" got home they had a drink. Robert, as if warned by his instinct, had an eager affectionate smile. He helped her with her coat, put away her gloves, running in and out of her room like a husband; he held her chair for her. They began laughing.

"Robert, this is just like old times."

She blushed as she remembered her traffic with the Princess.

"Yes, by Jove. I half expect Rollo to drop in. Do you remember incidentally that chap from Kaula Lumpur, big red-faced chap? I never told you, I had a bothering experience with him. Nothing came of it fortunately."

"Oh, I think I do, Robert."

"You remember, he brought with him this fellow with a lot of medals who told me we were quite done out there in the East. I believed him, too. It was my party, remember? And he kept paying for rounds of drinks. I felt very shoddy, not right. But this chap decided me. That was the day I decided to pack up and go. And you see, he was right: we are done out there in the East."

"But all these terrible wars, Robert?"

"Those are parting shots to cover our retreat."

"Yes, I wish we were still there. That was our life."

The next morning the Princess, looking down from her hotel window at about ten in the morning, was somewhat surprised to see Robert and Lilia crossing the public square hand in hand and walking together with the unmistakable trotting and nodding of the long married. She dismissed this incident from her mind. She had made up her mind to save Lilia before she set out for the Paris clinic.

They were saying:

"I always admired you, Lilia."

"Men did admire me when I was a girl. I never can understand why it was you."

"But it was."

"But you really took it so complacently, Robert."

"Not so complacently. I was upset when you ran off like that yesterday."

"You knew quite well I was with the Princess."

"The Princess is an interferer. She influences you."

"She is a very good-hearted woman. I won't hear a word against her."

"Let's keep on walking. It's good for your health. Let's go along the lake. I like to see the gulls, they swoop and circle, what a noise their wings make!"

"I often thought the swooping of the angels would be deafening, after I heard the noise these gulls make. I should not like to hear the swooping down of all the angels. I should go deaf. I'd fall on my face, cover my ears. Doomsday would be funny to see, Robert. I hope I see it. With the wings coming down so thick you could see no sky. Supposing it were here on the lake!"

"Well, yes, if you like, but it's a gloomy idea. Do you want to sit in the kiosk? They put up a glass kiosk and there's no use for it. Who wants to sit in a glass kiosk? Do you remember last spring when the gulls would not take our bread? I met a chap whose brother is an ornithologist. He says the birds gather out there and then they are on their way to Norway. I don't know why they don't eat when they are on their way to Norway. There must be stopping places on the way."

"Let's go along the lake a little and then turn in by that diagonal street. There's a house there that seems painted, because of the Virginia creeper right across the wall. I like painted walls, as they have in Italy."

"Well, yes, if you like: but why not stay here."

"Robert, and you such a great one for walking!"

"Let's shelter in the kiosk. There's a bit of a *bise* today."

"I wondered why I seemed to have a little headache."

"Now, Lilia, let's have no more of that headache today."

"But, dear, it is real."

"Then let us walk. It comes from not walking."

"Yes, you asked me to walk. It's a lovely morning, a lovely Sunday. I love Sundays; I feel more loved. I feel there are not so many troubles in the world."

"Well, that is just your idea."

"Yes, I know I shall be just as unhappy tomorrow."

"Why be unhappy, Lilia?"

"You know why, Robert. Don't let us talk about it."

"Very well; if you wish it."

"But you know so well that you could make me so happy."

"Don't you rather hug your misery? Come, let us walk a little way. If you don't cheer up, I'll have to get another wife."

"Don't use that word, Robert."

He burst out into frank laughter. She looked down.

"Well, yesterday you made me wait two hours for my tea and there wasn't any tea. I didn't know what had happened to you. I thought to myself, Well, Lilia has deserted me at last; now all I must do is to go and get a girl with long blonde hair. I love long blonde hair; it's nice to dance with. We'll go walking and we'll come home and talk—somewhere. I'll go to New York, if Lilia has left me, I'll go to Alassio, or to Marrakesh and get a society blonde; or a bambina in Italy and all night we'll just take a walk, sit on the beach, in the starlight. You know, like we did in Tahiti that year? You remember that weekend? We motored out, and when we got to the end of the beach someone asked for a ride? Remember how fast we went? We thought it was a holdup! You were so late yesterday, I didn't know what had happened. I thought you had got under a car."

"Robert, you know you are only teasing me. I won't go any farther. I have to meet the Princess."

She turned away.

"Lilia!"

She turned back.

"Lilia, come and kiss me; don't be such a silly girl."

She came back to him: "Well, if you wish it, Robert; but it doesn't mean anything. You have lost me. I'll kiss you, but it's finished. I've been meaning to tell you. I loved you, I was loyal to you, and there never was another man for me. But you have lost me. You let me down, Robert. I've been waiting and praying the last few years, for some way to get out of it. These two or three years."

Robert kissed her and said:

"You foolish girl. Where will you find someone better for you than me? Where will you find him?"

"Oh, I won't find anyone, Robert. There isn't anyone. I must just go and leave you and be miserable the rest of my life."

He started after; but she begged him to stay behind. He stood looking after her and then began walking up and down, puzzled and anxious. At last he sat in the glass kiosk looking in all directions. He said to himself:

"It's that interfering Princess."

But he went to lunch with her as arranged.

The Princess had brought Angel with her.

"Then you and I can take a little walk afterwards, Robert; I want to discuss some plans with you."

They began with aperitifs at eleven-thirty and had a delightful luncheon ordered beforehand by the Princess. This took place at a small restaurant called the Lake Club, which had once been a kiosk and had been turned into a pretty, lively dining place by an enterprising cook, a Monsieur Raoul Raymond who had once been a chef on the railways. The Princess was amusing, calling the Soviets "Asia and Tramps Incorporated," and telling them people relied upon her for everything, racetrack touts, stock exchange tips, black-market places if they went abroad, the best cabins on boats. They told her their favorite anecdotes, forgetting how many of them she had heard before.

Mr. Wilkins said: "I wrote to that man in Alassio I mentioned, to ask if the lira was still a buy; and meantime I heard from a man in Kuala Lumpur about our business there. He is sending a man to see me about the rubber business, but I very much fear he is going to tell me what I know already. I don't mind doing a stroke of business now and then; in fact, I must be continually in business to get the rest of my money out of the East; but it really is strange the things business people expect you to do."

The Princess said: "I really don't understand why you don't go and live in my house in Venice. It's on a canal and I simply have no use for it. Part of Lilia's objection to living here, Robert, is that you have no friends and have nowhere to receive any."

"But, Bili, I don't feel like taking a whole house. I have never lived with anyone. You know, in the East I lived at first in a chummery, but after my friend left I moved away to bachelor quarters and found out I was a natural bachelor. Odd, eh? I suppose it is in one."

"Well, why don't you take a brace of apartments in that Alassio place in that case? You could be separate and together.

You would live a private life and be together without the publicity of a hotel. Lilia is such a dear girl; I am so fond of Lilia. And she is a shrinking sort of woman, Robert."

"Oh, everyone is fond of Lilia: she has the art of making friends."

Lilia said: "You are talking about me as if I were not here. I am going to church to pray to my saint and I hope this time he will tell me what to do. I will see you for drinks, Robert."

"Oh, don't—" said Robert, rising; then he sank back. "I know I cannot stop Lilia going to church."

"And now, Robert, let us have a little chat. Let's have some more coffee and some brandy. You see, Robert, though you call yourself her cousin, everyone knows the situation and it is an absurd one. Don't say anything. I am going to have my say."

"Did Lilia know you were going to have your say?"

"She knew and she forbade me. But for me, I am fond of arranging things for people that they can't do for themselves, and I feel sorry for dear Lilia, such a dear natural woman. You know how she feels about her children's estrangement?"

Mr. Wilkins laughed easily. "Oh, I shouldn't bother too much about that. It's Madeleine, I'm sure. She's a spoiled brat but a nice girl, she'll come round. Her mother must simply stand firm. If I had had the arranging of her affairs, I should have had Madeleine married long ago. I am afraid Madeleine is a little like me. I was fond of the children as children, I suppose there is a lot of me in them. Children are imitative. I know those children, Princess; I held them on my knee."

"Yes, Lilia said you were like a father or an uncle to them."

"Oh, I am afraid I was not like a father to them. I have led a selfish life, Princess; entirely for myself. Whether it was good or bad for me I can't say. I lived for myself. Lilia's children were the only bright spots in my life. I think I can say I was not selfish about them. I liked to visit them and bring them toys. I could wield safety pins and that sort of thing. I gave them treats. I won't say I never spent my money on others. I've made a loan or two, not always to the most reliable sort of chap, and I've wagered a bit and even played cards a bit; and I've spent a bit of money on short ones and small gins and little dinners at the club, and naturally when my turn came round I always gave a party; and I was always chummy with people and paid my scot; but I'm selfish in the sense that I never did marry and I'm not sure I ever wanted to. My money came and went. Naturally I kept some; but I was responsible to no one. That is what I don't like—being conscious of a responsibility to someone. Then I should feel my selfishness very acutely. You see I was very selfish. Oh, don't mistake me, Bili, you can do nothing with me. I am a selfish man."

"Still, I am going to take Lilia's part; there is no need to put her case. Every servant in the hotel, even old Charlie, could tell you that you are doing wrong."

"Old Charlie!" He laughed.

"Oh, don't snap me up; everyone knows that Charlie has a mistress in the South of France who kept him for years under the occupation and that he won't go near her to marry her; and that he takes little girls up to a room in that horrible fleabag; but he's a respectable man just the same. And you are not respectable, Robert. You can easily get married here, secretly, never telling your mother and sisters; it can last for years. You will not suffer; I am sure Lilia will be no burden to you; and she will stay here and bring out her money."

"Oh, she will bring out her money, my dear Bili. I am seeing to that."

"You are crowing too soon. But Robert, I must go up to Lausanne; will you walk Angel part of the way with me?"

"Oh, no; I must take my nap. It's a new habit I've developed and I don't seem able to do without it. I'll see you this evening at the Café Grand Palace."

Mrs. Trollope came home from church looking very tired. She was troubled that she had had no answer from her saint; and she worried about Madame Blaise, who would be angry that they were spending so much time with the Princess.

She came home at five o'clock, at which time Madame Blaise was usually in the Old English Tea Room, having tea and cakes. But no sooner did she enter her room than Madame Blaise knocked on the wall; and in a moment they both appeared at her door, Dr. Blaise with a remarkable twinkle in his eye. He said:

"You see, I decided to stay the week and take a little holiday for once; and then I am taking my wife home with me."

They were dressed to go out. The doctor invited Mrs. Trollope and Mr. Wilkins for cocktails at about six-thirty, then to dinner and to a cabaret or dancing place. Leave it all to him, he said; he would fix it up. Madame Blaise also seemed to be in the best of humors. Mrs. Trollope was very much embarrassed and went in to consult Robert. Robert said:

"Tell them we shall be delighted. We'll meet them here. And I shall fix it up with Bili—I shall tell her—yes, I shall tell her my sister is coming." He laughed in delight.

"Your sister!"

He laughed. "Since it is so unlikely, she must believe it. And I should like to miss Bili and the Angel this evening."

They accepted, and the Blaises then went off arm in arm and began laughing heartily, the doctor shouting with laughter as they reached the lobby. Mrs. Trollope was disturbed, then shocked. What could it mean? However, she told Mr. Wilkins that she had been wrong, the Blaises were in a good mood and wanted to pay them back in the grand manner for the entertainment of the other evening. She said: "I think better of them; I had the queer idea they would do us some hurt."

Mr. Wilkins laughed, scolded Lilia for her imagination, "always worrying about insults and offenses," and said he supposed that Dr. Blaise, one of the best-known doctors in Switzerland, would have some mental balance and social nous; he was not to be judged by his wife. Lilia must have noticed that what she said often didn't make sense.

"We must be charitable, Robert: she is a drug addict, though in a small way. She merely takes it to steady her nerves and she is in the doctor's care."

She sat down to drink with Robert, ruminating.

"But, Robert, what do you make of it? He was so coarse in the café that night, saying, 'I am a slave and so are you;' and saying that had decided to live separately and she would never see the Basel house again. We decided, you know, that he had caught her in some situation—she talks so much about gigolos. Though it seems unlikely. Though she said to me once, 'My son is my only gigolo.' But there they were arm in arm like thief and—h'm—and thief and laughing loudly at the whole world. She told me only yesterday that she was never going back there; yet the day before she invited me to stay there. And now he says she is going back."

"Oh, they have made it up. And I believe, Lilia, that people tell you fairy tales to see your eyes pop open. They see you are gullible. They had a quarrel and now it is made up. You are always so imaginative, Lilia; it is one of your feminine traits. It is the kind of thing that men like, but it would never do in business. By the by, the Princess has taken to lecturing me about you, I am not sure it is not without your consent. I can do without another curtain lecture this evening."

Mrs. Trollope said nothing. Mr. Wilkins telephoned the Princess. They had to be careful. The Princess lived near enough to mark their comings and goings. Mr. Wilkins said that one of his sisters, the very old one, was coming from Yorkshire that night to stay in Montreux; and that they both had to go to the station to see her to her hotel and see that she had some dinner. She was an old-style Englishwoman who had never been abroad and would rather be with her own family; and in fact was only coming to make sure she had a place in Robert's will.

He laughed to Lilia: "The Princess will understand that; and she will think we are all being reconciled and so I shall hear no more about marrying you. Do you know that Bili has actually consulted a lawyer about it?"

Lilia said she would go to church tomorrow and beg to be forgiven for this lie.

They changed their clothes and were ready by six-thirty. Mr. Wilkins was called to the telephone in the office and came back looking rather pale and stiff; he also looked as if he had had a revelation. He said:

"Really, Lilia, really, you will not have to go to church tomorrow to talk about the lie. Let us have a short one before the Blaises get here. I have seen the long arm of coincidence operate, but by Jove I turned cold at this one. I shall believe in table turning. That was a long-distance telephone call from my sister Flo. She is using up her travel allowance to come to Switzerland with her old school friend, Miss Price. I think they met at a young ladies' establishment on the south coast about fifty years ago; and they are coming here, not to Montreux, but here, tomorrow, by the midnight train. Oh, my aunt!"

"What for, in heaven's name?"

Mr. Wilkins said in anxious tones: "If I knew, Lilia, I should tell you. Still, I am glad we did not tell a lie. Or only half of one. *I can call spirits from the vasty deep;* yes, and when I call them, they do come."

He slapped his knee. "Oh, by James, that's ripe. I had a Scots grandmother, but as for second sight—"

They had their short ones and he became serious, thinking his own thoughts and leaving Lilia to think hers, which could not be pleasant. He poured two more short ones. Lilia felt her headache coming back; she felt wretched indeed.

"Oh, I don't know if I can spend a whole evening with the Blaises; they are such bores, and ugly people. He has no small talk and she is always talking about her son. I wish I could see the Princess. It is going to be very difficult here for me, Robert, unless Flo has become reconciled and is coming here to make friends."

"Oh, that is not it. Flo does not know you are here. She thinks I am here alone. She does not know we are traveling together."

He finished his drink and remarked: "Do you know, that woman is a good card player if I remember aright. We could have some games."

"Is she going to stay here?"

"Oh, of course not. I shall make arrangements tomorrow. She will never come here. I shall see to that. I shall find out how long she is staying and I may move to her hotel just for the few days; it would be more prudent."

"And I am to stay here alone?"

"Surely you don't want to meet Flo?"

It was seven. The Blaises had not returned. Where were they supposed to meet them? There was no message downstairs; and the Blaises had mentioned in the office that they were driving to Clarens to a friend's house for dinner; the friend was a colleague of the doctor.

Robert and Lilia changed their clothes and went down quietly to the dining room, examining their memories; they had made a mistake somehow. Mrs. Trollope's headache was very bad; and after dinner she said:

"Oh, I believe I shall go and see the Princess. I can tell her about your sister; and we can meet Bili after all at the café, as Flo is coming tomorrow."

"One thing I don't care for in you, Lilia, is that you are so clinging. If you are dropped by Madame Blaise you must run straight to the Princess for consolation."

"I am not dropped by Madame Blaise; it is a misunderstanding," said Lilia, frightened.

"My opinion is, you may take it with a grain of salt, that that was a deliberate sell."

"Oh, you are too suspicious. Gliesli loves me, she calls me her Liliali; she would never hurt me. And why should Dr. Blaise lend himself to such a thing?"

"I think he is a very peculiar man."

"You look so conceited when you smirk like that."

Robert said: "It is because I think I am clever. I have ideas about Dr. Blaise that could not be put into print and I am not going to breathe to you."

After dinner they sat for a while upstairs and then decided to go for a walk. They had scarcely reached the footpath when they met Dr. and Madame Blaise strolling along arm in arm, just as if waiting for them. The Blaises said goodnight coolly, politely, but, it seemed to Mrs. Trollope, with malicious smiles, though it was hard to tell in the starlight. When they left once more, the Blaises broke into immoderate laughter.

They went to the Lake Club for a drink. Lilia's heart beat hard.

"Oh, Robert, I cannot understand it."

"I can. They took it out of us for being what we are. They took it out of us for putting up with their boorishness."

"Where's the sense?"

"If you want my plain idea about the doctor, Lilia, the man has all the making of a criminal. I should not be at all surprised to see his name in the papers one day."

"And you say I am imaginative! All on account of a mistaken invitation."

"I am never wrong in this kind of intuition, if that is what you call it," said Robert.

"You are right about wrong things, I know. Oh, the world must not be this way."

They had a long conversation with a waitress they knew about Bogota and about Newfoundland, when "Oh, Robert!" said Mrs. Trollope. The swing doors opened, the circular door rotated and in came the Blaises. The Blaises saw them but pretended not to, and went to another part of the room, where they were hidden—in fact, to a favorite corner usually occupied by Lilia and Robert.

"Are they expecting us?" said Lilia, but at this moment into the café from the hotel came a tall dark woman with a young man at her side. Both were showily dressed. Everyone knew about this woman. She was the widow of the richest man in that part of Switzerland, owned factories, all kinds of establishments, had a share in the luxurious hotel in which the café was situated. The woman and her lover joined the Blaises.

"Oh, this is going too far!" said Mrs. Trollope. After a reasonable time, Lilia and Robert went back to the hotel.

At one-thirty in the morning someone knocked on Robert's door and asked him to call Madame Blaise to go down to the office and answer a long-distance call from New York, from her son. Charlie was off duty, and Herman the German as they called him, the man from Lucerne, refused to understand where the guests' rooms were. Robert's was at the head of the stairs, and him he called. "Madame Blaise is there," said Robert. The man shrugged in his ox-like manner, said "Weiss nicht" and turned to the stairs. Then Robert thought that the lady might be with her husband, so he said to Herman the German, "Der Doktor—the doctor is in the end room." "Weiss garnichts davon," said Herman and went downstairs. Well, thought Robert to himself, I am not calling on that bundle of charms; and he knocked on Lilia's door with the message. After noises like a horse struggling in dreams in his stall, Mrs. Trollope came out onto the landing, and then Madame Blaise herself. She had bundled herself into several extra pieces of underclothing, a wrapper and her fur coat, and tied a scarf round her head, with her hat on top of it; and while dressing she shouted at Mrs. Trollope that Lilia had no thought for her at all, she knew that Gliesli's grandmother had died of tuberculosis and thought of nothing but her own selfish whims, that she was a tiresome little woman, a hotel pest, and that Madame Blaise did not know why she had left her beautiful home, not cold like this death trap, but heated, like a hothouse, not packed with hotel rats from the mountains but full of efficient servants, where everything was done for her hand and foot, to come and live with ridiculous English exiles in the cheapest hotel in a tedious French-Swiss resort. She said to her husband who had come in from his room:

"You are French-Swiss too and absolutely intolerable, dirty and inefficient; and the French and the English anyhow are the laughing-stock of Europe. Everyone knows the English are a fallen nation; and you know it, too, Trollope and Wilkins, cousins who sleep together, or you would not be hiding here like cowards, misers, insects that you are, lower than the hotel rats of whom you make friends, rich people and grudging every penny, going shabby. I am tired of your company."

"Come to the phone, Liesl," said the doctor.

"And you want to expose me to the cold and you grudge me every penny; you push me out of sight here in a rubbishy little pension, so that you can eat and drink all you please on my money and sleep with the servants."

"Come on, Liesl!"

"I will go. I think it will be better if I go home. I am rudely treated, treated like dirt, a woman like me—"

She picked up her crocodile handbag to take it with her, put her hand into it and suddenly pushed her open palm at Lilia.

"I present you with the five francs my dinner cost you. We are used to good living. Do you think we didn't see how you grudged us every mouthful?"

She went downstairs. They heard her coming up a few minutes later saying:

"I am shivering, Blaise; it's terribly cold. I am utterly wretched here. I must go home."

"Yes, you had better go home. But now you had better go to bed. Everyone wants to sleep."

He said goodnight to Lilia and Robert in an affable way with the same odd twinkle and a sharp stern sidelong glance which had been an expression of his ever since the night of the dinner.

"I have a most disagreeable impression, most," said Mr. Wilkins, in a low tone.

Mrs. Trollope was in bed crying,

"And all because we did not invite them to lunch. They are greedy. I could not show so much greed," said Lilia in a voice which she intended Madame Blaise to hear. Madame Blaise knocked on the wall, and called:

"Let people sleep."

Lilia wept.

The result of all this was that Madame Blaise went off with Dr. Blaise in his car the next morning to live in the home which she had quit seven months before and which she had sworn never to set foot in again. When she left Madame Blaise kissed Lilia, took her by both hands, begged her pardon. "I was tired and nervous and cold and frightened, the doctor had been roaming round his room all night and I thought he meant me harm."

She told Mrs. Trollope that when she returned after a few months she was going to stay at a charming hotel up the street, The Old English, recommended to her by some Russian ladies, White Russian, of course. It was very warm, pretty, and not much dearer than the Hotel Swiss-Touring; and she wanted Lilia to go there too.

"Perhaps, Liliali, I shall come back in a week and we shall all move there and sing Happy days are here again. We will show the Bonnards that we are not such fools as they take us for. Then, dear Liliali, for people in our position, it is not quite right to live in the most rundown hotel in town. Now promise me, if I do not come back in a week, you must come to live with me. We will be sisters. You will look after me and be a witness if the doctor tries to poison me."

She said this with the doctor looking on and smiling his odd smile; she kissed Lilia affectionately. They went out to the car. Madame Blaise said:

"Liliali, I shall write to you every day. Now mind you write to me. Forgive me, darling. You are my best friend. Remember, it is your duty. I impose it on you. You must live for me, when I am away, for I shall be so lonely without you. And remember, do not go to Paris or anywhere till I come back. Do not move till I come back, then we will all go to the Old English. If you are not there, there will be no charm for me there. Remember you are my only confidante; you know everything. You know all about him—" she pointed to her husband; "I adore you, Liliali, you owe it to me to wait for me here. And if I do not write, remember, you must come over to Basel and find out why. It will mean I am in danger."

So they parted. Mrs. Trollope did not like this parting. She told Mr. Wilkins that she thought it overbearing, not to say impertinent of "the old lady" to imagine that she would wait for her there, "tied hand and foot."

But Mr. Wilkins said; "Oof! I am glad she is gone; that is something to be thankful for. If I had only known before. Now I know how to manage her—deprive her of a meal."

"Don't speak that way of a poor woman who goes in fear of her husband."

Mr. Wilkins laughed.

"If I only knew what you were thinking, Robert. At times you seem to me a complete stranger. I am living with a stranger."

"We all are," said Mr. Wilkins and laughed.

He went up the hill to reserve two rooms in the Old English Hotel for his sister and her old friend Miss Price. When he came back, he said:

"Well, you had better keep out of the way, Lilia. I shall do my level best to keep them from here. I decided I could not stay with them, after all. I shall eat with them, take them on trips, take them to the Casino and they will be satisfied. I shall not allow them to come prying round here. Of course, Lilia, if you should see me out with them, you had better make believe you do not know me."

Lilia went up to see the Princess. She meant to tell her everything. But when she got there the Princess was packing; very flustered and irate. She had to go to Paris at once; there had

135

been a mistake, she was to go into the clinic at once. She said to Lilia, as soon as she saw her, that she must take Angel; and she gave her the address of the lawyer she had been seeing on Lilia's case.

"And I have had such stupid letters from Ramon, my fiancé. He thinks he can do anything with me. He is so lazy. Why do I have to meet such a lazy man, when I am full of energy? He does not want to open a restaurant; he wants to have a good time. And what else do you think he wants? Where is it? *Mi salud y la de mi madre*—no, he thinks I am worrying about his health! *Seria un ladron.* Yes, I must send him some more money; he was with someone who must have been a thief. Yes, yes, here it is, such impudence! He wants me generously and nobly to pay for the fare of a cousin of his, *una señorita de veinte y dos anos*, a young lady of twenty-two. I know those cousins!"

She stopped and said to Lilia; "I beg your pardon, Lilia. But I am in such a fit of temper, my head is on fire. And yet he is so sweet to me. 'I miss you, you are only a child,' he says to me; 'you are so much older, I respect you for all you are, and yet with me you are a child and I feel all the tenderness I would feel for a child. In life you are a child.'"

The Princess hastily wiped her eyes.

"And so, Lilia, you must take Angel, take him to the Blaises. I myself, to tell the turth, telephoned the clinic and they called me back; for it is urgent. You see he is becoming interested in women younger than himself."

"And now I am going to be quite alone," said Lilia, sitting down.

"Will you take Angel?"

"Oh, yes, I promised, didn't I? But what on earth will Robert say?"

"You had better take him straight to Basel."

"I should take him to England, if they would let him in; but there is that quarantine."

"Oh, no, Angel must never be in quarantine; he would die of loneliness."

Mrs. Trollope took the lawyer's address, though she knew she would never use it. She went back to the hotel leading Angel. Mr. Wilkins was resting and asked her to go in and see what "that poltergeist" wanted. Mrs. Trollope tied Angel to the bedpost in her room and went in.

Miss Chillard's flesh had sunk back onto her skeleton.

"I am afraid you are not well, Miss Chillard. Shall I send for the doctor?"

"They have taken my money for the hotel. I cannot pay the doctor."

"Shall I make you some tea?"

"I cannot take anything. I have not eaten for three days, for these carrion-crows are only waiting for me to eat, to take the last of my money. They will put me out and you can see I cannot move. I do not know what is to become of me. I am dying. I don't want to die on the train home, in a dusty third-class carriage. If only I could see Zermatt once more, where I was happy, I would not mind dying. I want to die there. I don't want to die here, Mrs. Collop, Mrs. Collop! What am I to do?"

"My God, my God," said Mrs. Trollope to herself. She said to the invalid; "I will bring you some food and then I will go and pray for you." This is what she did; but the woman did not take the soup Mrs. Trollope had begged in the kitchen. She glanced at it indifferently and said: "The smell of it makes me sick; throw it down the sink, please."

Mrs. Trollope took Angel in to Mr. Wilkins and went to the church, where she prayed for a long time for guidance and help for Miss Chillard. As she knelt there she heard money chinking somewhere and she thought of the money she had in her bag, the thousands of francs from the safe.

"I will do one good deed and perhaps I will be forigven for leaving Robert."

She went back to the hotel, and although she heard Robert calling her and Angel barking she went in to Miss Chillard, and said to her: "Miss Chillard, I have had a message from my saint and I am going to give you the money to go to Zermatt. If you get there can you manage?"

"They can put me out dying at the station. I do not care once I am there. For me it is heaven and earth; that is where heaven opens for me. I was happy there, I never knew what happiness was till then."

Her large sunken eyes burned. She put out a weak hand to thank Mrs. Trollope or perhaps to take the money. Her voice was weak, hardly audible, and her touch was weaker than a leaf.

Mrs. Trollope went down to Mrs. Bonnard to ask if there was a way of getting Miss Chillard to the station. The hotel keeper was very glad to get rid of her, very anxious about her; for she looked as if she would die there; so she arranged what she could.

Miss Chillard, supported by Charlie and Mrs. Bonnard and Mrs Trollope, was just able to walk out of the hotel and to the station.

"I am afraid she will die in the train," said Mrs. Trollope to Mrs. Bonnard.

When the train came in, they found her an unoccupied compartment and put in some of her bundles; for she could not take all of her luggage. She said:

"I wanted this so much! I never thought it would happen. That place was my heaven."

"Goodbye, goodbye!" She did not answer.

"And now, dear Madame Bonnard, I must tell you that I am leaving you too," said Mrs. Trollope when we returned to the hotel; and said that she was leaving the next morning for Basel. She had sent a telegram from the station. "If Miss Chillard is going to heaven, I am sure I am going to hell, for that's where it seems to me the Doctor and Gliesli live; but I am going there; I am not waiting on Robert's pleasure here. I am sorry, Madame Bonnard, you have been so good, a sister. But my position is more than false. I can never bring him to his senses. I haven't the sense myself, I suppose."

"Are you really leaving him?" I asked.

"Yes. I think he wants me to. He doesn't know it himself. But it is his old age that is coming on; and he always was a bachelor. You see how he is rushing off to play cards with his old sister?"

Mrs. Trollope was crying; but she wiped her eyes.

"I am crying and I will be crying, I know. But it is no use. I am grateful for what I had. I had a true love. I can never be angry with him. I must leave you. I am sorry. It is beautiful here. And I am sorry to leave my loved ones, Luisa and dear Charlie and you dear Madame and dear little Olivier. Bless you all."

Mr. Wilkins sat alone at his table. He no longer read the newspapers and magazines which had annoyed Mrs. Trollope. He no longer went for his constitutional along the promenade; nor went up to his room after lunch to nap with his handkerchief over his face. He wanted to keep Mrs. Trollope's room, but she was not there to pay for it herself, and he would not pay for it; so it was easy for me to explain to him that the spring season was beginning and that I intended to put two beds into the room; the room would cost double. I said that his own room too might one day be wanted as a two-bed room, but added:

"Since you and your wife are such good old clients, I will leave your room as it is for a while, until the busy season."

"My cousin and I," said he.

It was out of courtesy that I called Mrs. Trollope his wife; for she was, indeed. Why was he so afraid of the word? Other unmarried couples in the hotel were very pleased to be called husband and wife.

The Princess said: "Oh, I know him; it is because he is afraid of common-law marriage."

"But we don't have that here," I said.

"It's something of the sort."

"But why is he afraid to acknowledge his cousin, as he calls her? He is not married."

"Oh, he is not married. Depend upon it, it is something to do with money. He is very greedy. Perhaps the old hag can cut him out of the estate if she wants."

"What old hag?"

"Why his mother of course. His father was rich, a leader of the community; he must have left it all to the mother and she tied a noose round all their necks."

"Is that true?"

"I know nothing about such wretched people," said the Princess.

Before she went, she gave Robert several curtain lectures; but he had little time for her and avoided her. It was easy for him. All his time was spent with his sister Flo and Miss Price, who were staying at the Old English.

The old ladies had got Mr. Wilkins into an almost perpetual card game at this hotel. For a short time the White Russian who ran the card club, a Monsieur Nemazashto, had operated his little club in our hotel. It became so popular that he needed more space. He could be seen very often along the promenade or the principal lakeside street, very busy, with a large tram-conductor's cashbag on a canvas strap slung over his shoulder. Mr. Wilkins seemed pleased by the new company, though he assured his friends that the old ladies were overstaying their time and their resources, and though it was intended as a raid on his cash he was not going to let them damage his assets. He came home each evening the first week radiant with his success at cards; he must have been a very good player. He won from his sister and Miss Price. He could not wait to rush out again after dinner to the Old English Hotel, to join them again. When did any of them see the Lake?

When I asked him friendlily about the game, he said:

"Oh, I am enjoying myself, Madame. I am thankful that my cousin is not here. She would be very lonely and I could not take her with me of course. It would create a fearful scandal; and how thankful I am that interfering woman has left." He meant the Princess. He continued:

"It is really a new life for me. My cousin does not care for cards. Now it happens that I have always been very handy with the cards and, touch wood, I have good luck usually; and if not, I can turn a bad card into a fairly good one."

When the Princess left she cautioned him about his new life:

"You are retreating from life more and more, Robert. You will not face any issue. Lilia is an issue: she is human. But you prefer a dream world."

He said: "But I rather think that if Lilia had played cards I should not have got into these lazy habits."

The Princess said; "Lilia is not a great gambler. I am. But not with cards. Life can only be played for big stakes. Lilia for you is a big stake; and you will lose her."

He said: "Oh, Lilia will never leave me; she does not know life. I have always managed for her. Life would terrify Lilia, without me. As you say, she is not a gambler."

The Princess left for Paris. Mr. Wilkins had a few letters from Mrs. Trollope; and when I asked after her he said:

"I am afraid she has made a mistake: they are not people one can live with."

Madame Blaise sent for all her luggage. This relieved my mind. I had not known what to do about their rooms. I had written to Dr. Blaise and Madame, but had never had a reply. I wrote another letter to Mrs. Trollope asking about their plans. She sent me a letter at once, saying:

> My dear Selda,
>   I wish I could talk to you, you have seen so much, though you are so young and you understand people without criticizing them. This is no place to stay, I am very unhappy. But I am a temporizer. I know when I leave here I must face a new, empty life. I know I will find some trifles to fill it with and I have my religion

and my dear children, who say they will take me back as soon as I make a clean break with Mr. Wilkins. I think I have made a break, and I have suffered a little, dear Selda; but Mr. Wilkins will not believe me. I have been so weak in the past, I do not blame him. As for coming back—I am not coming back. I am glad you have rearranged my room. About the house here, I am so troubled. One cannot be sure. Some days, Dr. Blaise and his wife seem so friendly and I can imagine them going back to you for some summer weeks. At other times, dreadful things are said. I am a guest here and must not be a spy and informer, though they are very open, and do not seem to care. I am, alas, a "witness" as Madame Blaise said I should be. I am quite afraid and much embarrassed. But when I say I am going, Madame Blaise begs me to stay; "you are my only defender and my only witness," she says. I think she is a neurotic, perhaps; but she is unhappy. People suffer and we call them names; but all the time they are suffering. I know I am not clever: it is partly because I cannot believe that life is meant to be ugly. I cannot understand the position of the housekeeper here, Selda. If you were here you would understand at once. One cannot imagine that she attracts Dr. Blaise; and she seems to be close, even too close, to Madame Blaise. She helps her, does things for her, lets her have things that the doctor forbids her to have. But there is a bad feeling. Madame Blaise says it is because of that woman that she left home, that is Ermyntrud; and then she says she could never leave Ermyntrud again, that she is her safeguard. How can I be her only defender and her witness? Against whom and about what? I like to do what I am asked if it is in my power; I feel it is a message, that my saints are talking to me and that they will look after me. But, for one thing, Ermyntrud, the housekeeper, is very unpleasant to me; she was from the beginning. I was very sorry for her, because she is a servant and very often they both, when they are getting on well, treat her like a dog from the street; and then—but I don't understand people, Selda. I will say no more. I do not really think you are to blame if you let their rooms. They did not answer you. But of course, I cannot ask them if they are going back to the *hotel. I can only tell you about myself. I was warned by someone long ago, that if I did not make a life for myself, but remained so dependent on Mr. Wilkins, I should be very sorry later on, "when it is too late." I am not sorry; though I know it is very late; but with the help of those I always can depend on, I am going to strike out for myself now. How strange we must seem to you, Selda, in your hardworking busy life? I wish I had a life as busy. I will write to you from England. Do not tell Mr. Wilkins yet that I am going there. I don't know what day yet; but it will be soon. And then if he wants to, he can follow me. I feel sure he will not. I hoped for it at first. As the days pass, I feel sure he will not; and I am beginning at last to hope that he will not. Love to Olivier and my regards to your dear husband.*

Your friend,
Lilia Trollope

However, Mrs. Trollope must have written to Mr. Wilkins that day; for the next morning Mr. Wilkins was very disturbed. He asked me if I had had a letter from his cousin about her room and I said yes, she was not keeping it on.

"Well, I am staying on," he said; and then I told him that he would be charged double for the summer season; it always was so. He said that I should wait till the other rooms were taken before "this holdup"; and he said the town was not even half full, the great hotels along the lake were empty. I said: "But that is all changed now, Mr. Wilkins. These days are gone. It was the British who used to stay here in villeggiatura; now they have not the money. The Americans and French all run through in their cars; they do not even stay one night. Now those hotels are being taken over by the trades unions for their members and taken up in block bookings by the travel agencies. They are being converted as holiday centers. This means that we who remain will be doing a splendid business forever for those few people who want to stay."

He said he was most certainly not going to stay here alone; and he wrote at once to Mrs. Trollope to come back to us. She did not answer. She had already left for London. He wrote to Madame Blaise about her plans; but in reply all he had was a newspaper cutting which said that Madame Blaise had died of

142

heart disease and that her entire estate, except for two settlements, had been left to the housekeeper Ermyntrud, if she married Dr. Blaise. No doubt a wedding took place.

"I do not know what I am going to do without Mrs. Trollope," said Mr. Wilkins, when he came down to pay for his room. He continued:

"She should never have left me. I arranged my affairs to include her and she knew it quite well. This has upset all my calculations. I shall have to reorientate my whole plans. It is most inconsiderate; but she never had any ballast. At the same time, I shall not go to England. I should have to return all the capital they allowed me to bring out; I shall certainly not do that; and for her sake I shall keep hers here too. She does not know what trouble she is in for, having to explain why she exported capital and then came home without it. She is going to write to me to help her out of the pickle. But I shall say simply, Lilia, you must come abroad again."

He went on talking, but at this moment there was some trouble going on in the foyer. The Admiral was going upstairs to her room. She had brought the lift down, she went in and tried to slam the door. She could not get used to the electric eye and wanted it taken out. She thought she might be trapped in there. She shouted:

"The lift is out of order, I can't slam the door."

"She can't see that it is closing," said Mr. Wilkins.

One of my lodgers, a young man, Mr. Forel, who was sitting in his shirt sleeves writing a letter in the writing room, rushed out and shouted in French:

"Let it close and don't slam it! It's a mechanism; it can't be managed by brute force, brute force!"

The Admiral started to come out. "It's out of order; eh, l'homme!"

Mr. Forel exclaimed: "Animal, faut pas le forcer."

A young man coming down the stairs from the little rooms upstairs shouted suddenly, turning red, to Mr. Forel:

"Back into your hole, dog!"

"What were those words? Repeat them!" said the shirt-sleeved man, creeping closer.

"Back into your hole, like a dog," remarked the other young man, calmly.

"Don't speak to a man like that," I said.

The man in shirt sleeves turned to me and raised his fists:

"Dirty spies! Dirty spies! Switzerland is full of nothing but foreign spies!"

"You dare!" said the other young man.

"She is a spy, no one else here," said Mr. Forel, looking furiously at the Admiral.

I said to the Admiral: "Take no notice; he's mad."

The young man cried: "Mad, am I? Mad—ah—I'll report it to the police."

He ran back for his jacket, while the other young man, running down to the door, said over his shoulder: "You do that and we'll all say you're mad. Enough!"

"Mad!" cried Mr. Forel. He ran to the door.

The other young man went racing out. "Goodbye!" he shouted laughing, as he ran up the little asphalt path to the gate.

"You'll hear from me," said Mr. Forel running after him.

"Mad, mad!" shouted the young man, running his hands through his flying hair, as he made off.

"Tas de coquins!" said Mr. Forel, running to the gate.

"Goodbye," shouted the other.

"Mr. Hops!" shouted Mr. Forel.

"Goodbye, madman!"

"Smuggler, smuggler!" said Mr. Forel.

Mr. Hops reached the turn in the road and disappeared, still running. Mr. Forel stood at the gate shaking his arm in the air. He came slowly back, his shirttails flying out from his trousers. He had his slippers on and a hole in one of his socks so large it could be seen for hundreds of yards, I am sure. He stood for a while in the cold breeze, thin and bent. After calling something unintelligible to Mr. Hops, he turned and came towards the front door splaying his large flat feet, putting them down as if they were broken at the ankles. He was a postman who had had a nervous breakdown and was staying in one of the little rooms at the top for a holiday.

Ah, yes, Mrs. Trollope did not return to the Hotel Swiss-Touring. She wrote several times from England telling me about the prices of things and how strange she found the people's manners; and I had a postcard from Mr. Wilkins in Rome, where he was looking for a business opportunity; and later another from Cape Town, where he had gone on business, asking me if I had had a word from his cousin. I do not know if they ever saw each other again.